"A tale of profound, irrevocable changes in the middle of America in the 1960s, as a sheltered, upper-middle-class teenager becomes transformed, not only in his own physical and spiritual self, but also in his awareness of class and race and forces of discrimination he'd never had a clue of before. The narrative is powerful in its solid simplicity and dramatic, quietly vivid events. Although the time is past, the novel is very much of the present."

> — Ellen Cooney, author of *One Night Two Souls Went Walking* and *Thanksgiving*

"This is a very lovely, clear-eyed book about a young man's dawning awareness of extraordinary men and women, as well as the hard realities, in a Midwestern town where he's grown up. A generous and moving evocation of people living in a world that's undergoing change, and the ways, some deeply compassionate, others coldly cruel, with which they move into the unknown."

> — Douglas Penick, author of *Journey of the North Star*

"The poignant tale of a teenager becoming a man over one summer in the 1960s as he learns lessons of love and evil in a small Midwestern town. The writing is lean and powerful."

> — Don Trowden, author of *Normal Family*

SUMMER OF LOVE AND EVIL

A Novel

by Michael Kinnamon

PUBLERATI

Cover design by William Oleszczuk

Trade Paperback ISBN: 978-0-9979137-5-0
Ebook ISBN: 978-0-9979137-6-7

Publerati donates a portion of all sales to help spread literacy. Please learn more at www.publerati.com

In memory of my teachers, Professor Anthony C. Yu and Professor Nathan A. Scott Jr., from whom I learned the power of literature to illuminate the lives of persons otherwise forgotten.

SUMMER OF LOVE AND EVIL

"We can only learn to love by loving."

— Iris Murdoch

"There is some soul of goodness in things evil, would men
observingly distill it out."

— Shakespeare

Chapter One

As a kid, Charles had called them the "tickly hills," these sharp drops on the roller coaster road from Lockwood to the Missouri border that leave a tingle in your stomach. His dad often laughed about people who say Iowa is flat. "They haven't been to this part of the state, that's for sure!"

If he had thought about it, Charles would have said he liked this landscape: the heavily-wooded hills with fields of corn and soybeans tucked in between. When someone asked *Where you from?*, this was the picture his mind conjured up. And yet, he had to admit, he didn't know the first thing about growing corn or soybeans. Last year at church camp, a counselor had whipped up adolescent faith by challenging the campers to consider working with the church in another country. *You're all from Iowa! You can help farmers in Kenya or wherever grow better crops.* Well, yes, he was from Iowa, but how all these things grew was pretty much a mystery to him. As far as he could remember, he had never even sat on a tractor.

There was undoubtedly a closer place to buy condoms, but Charles knew for sure he could get them from the machine on the bathroom wall of the truck stop not far over the state line. Even if a trucker saw him put his quarters into the machine and teased him, it wouldn't be someone he knew. He planned to get two, so he could practice putting one on.

He envisioned how the rest of the day, the third Saturday in May, would unfold. First, the graduation ceremony where he'd be cheered as valedictorian of Lockwood High, class of 1967. Maybe not cheered, but at least acknowledged. Then, the graduation dance in the over-decorated high school gym, although he and Nancy wouldn't stay long. She may have helped decorate the gym, even enlisted him to put up streamers, but hadn't they gone to enough of these school events over the past two years? And waiting beyond the dance was the *real* party at Randall's farm, because his parents were guaranteed to be gone and Randall knew where to get beer. He had even hinted at other procurements, although Charles wasn't exactly sure what he had in mind.

A car met him as he approached the top of a hill, appearing over the ridge without warning. The driver raised his index finger off the steering wheel, the local form of greeting between motorists. Charles realized he was going over sixty, which tingled his stomach and caused his father's Buick to bounce over seams and asphalt patches in the little-used road. Although in a hurry, he slowed to fifty.

After a beer or two or three, he would get Nancy alone and tell her it was time to go all the way. No, maybe he wouldn't say anything at all; he often talked too much at times like that and messed things up. He would just begin to unbutton her blouse—she was usually okay with that—but then he would keep going. Except she might still have on her dress from the dance, in which case he would have to improvise. He tried to picture her naked, but the image of the dress, with lots of fabric and what she told him was an overlay of lace kept getting in the way.

He crossed the state line and in less than ten minutes reached the east-west highway. On one corner of the intersection, with its flashing light—red in his direction, yellow in the other—was a fireworks stand, on another corner Don's Café and Tavern, and on the third the filling station with its diesel pumps for trucks and buses. He put two dollars of gas in the car, so there wouldn't be any question why he was using the restroom, which to his relief was empty. But then he found that the machine wanted three quarters per condom, not two, so he had to ask for change from the smiling girl at the counter. He pretended to survey the beef jerky supply, before sidling into the restroom, only to find it now crowded with loud-talking truckers. Finally, after slipping out and in again, he made his purchases and headed back to Lockwood.

Everyone called it the Stringville Road because it ran past what remained of a town abandoned a half-century ago, back when new machinery allowed for bigger farms (and fewer farmers), and automobiles allowed those who survived the changes to travel all the way to Lockwood for supplies. Charles zipped past the overgrown foundations of Stringville homes, clumped in the corner of a pasture. Past what his father, who seemed to know everyone in the county, called the Clyman place, even though the Robinsons had lived there for as long as Charles could remember. Past the pond where he once went fishing with his friend, Brent, until Brent's family had to move. Their house seemed occupied, he noticed, but the roof of the barn was partially collapsed, and vines crawled over faded paint. Past several farmhouses, separated from him by a drainage ditch and barking dogs.

Of course, she might not agree with his plans for the evening, but he would remind her that she had begged him to stay in Lockwood for the summer *to be with me*. Her words. He could have taken that job in the library on the Drake campus and gotten a head start on his freshman year. That's certainly what his mother wanted him to do. He had even told Mr. Blankenship that he wouldn't be around to work another summer in the shoe store on the square, until Nancy had said, "Stay with me for the summer, before we go to different universities." Those were her words. And so he had agreed to stay. But that didn't mean just making out at the drive-in in Mahaska!

The rest of the day, however, did not go as Charles had envisioned. The graduation itself was fine; people even cheered when the valedictorian was announced. And the dance started

4

out okay. But when he suggested they leave, Nancy resisted. "Don't you want to spend time here with our friends? It's sad! Don't you think it's sad? We've known Jack and Karen and Stephanie and all of them our whole lives, and now it's coming to an end!" There were even tears.

When they finally did get to the farm, there were only a couple of beers left, both of which Charles drank after Nancy refused when he offered her one. Just as she refused his attempts at seduction. Before he could begin his rehearsed speech about what he had given up to stay in Lockwood for the summer, Nancy declared that she was ready to go home. There was no need to make a big deal about graduation night, because, after all, they would probably see each other tomorrow. That led to a huge, weepy argument, during which she accused him of having only one thing on his mind, and he accused her of being too uptight or something, at the end of which he blurted out that maybe it was time for them to start dating other people. And, somehow, that was that. She cried silently, looking out the window of his father's Buick as he drove her home.

After driving aimlessly for several minutes, Charles quietly entered his parent's house through the back door, not because he was home too late, but because he was back so embarrassingly early. His whole summer up in smoke! He sat on his bed, staring at the tree branch outside his bedroom window, feeling exhausted but anything but sleepy.

Charles' family had moved to the big house on Chestnut Street when he was five, so it was really the only home he had known. He knew, because his father made a point of telling visitors, that the house was built in the years leading up to World War I out of brick brought in from Kansas City, with a foundation of white, hand-chipped stone. Charles told his friends that it's just two stories, but this didn't count the full, mostly finished basement or the large attic or spacious porch, with its round pillars, which his mother decorated with hanging plants in summer and wreaths at Christmas. And then the sunroom, as well as a patio, recently added to the back of the house.

Charles' bedroom on the second floor looked out on the expansive backyard, big as the grade-school playground (as Nancy had once pointed out), which now had two new stumps. "I found out this week," Charles' father told him on the morning of graduation, "that the big elm in the corner also has the disease. See all those yellow leaves? A bunch have fallen behind the utility shed, and I want you to rake them up. There are bags in the shed." His father chuckled and shook his head. "I'm going to have to drum up more legal business just to cover the cost of tree removal."

Charles' mother had come up behind them during this conversation and now wanted to know how Charles was supposed to do yardwork when he would be starting on the street crew on Monday, not to mention keeping up with his French and piano and generally getting ready for college. "Robert, you can

6

hire someone to pick up your leaves. These are his last months at home, at least for a while, and he already has more than enough to do."

On Sunday morning, Charles left the house without eating breakfast to avoid interrogation from his mother and, especially, his younger sister: "How did Nancy look in her dress with all that pretty lace?" "Were the decorations at the school as beautiful as Nancy said?" "Where did the two of you decide to go after the dance?" He walked the five blocks to the church by himself, planning to get there early enough to escape pre-worship small talk and find a seat away from his family, who would follow soon. It didn't work. Several older members— who, he forgot, were always early—were intent on congratulating the valedictorian, although the men couldn't do it without teasing. "I remember J.L. was top of our class," said one of them, loud enough for Charles to overhear, "and he didn't amount to a hill of beans." Charles tried to smile appropriately, and then headed for the corner of a back pew. If he looked prayerful, he told himself, others might leave him alone, maybe even think he was praying because he'd done something worthy of repentance.

Once they were all back home, his mother announced she didn't feel like fixing a big lunch, so they could fend for themselves. There was plenty of stuff for sandwiches, which suited Charles just fine given there was much on his mind he didn't feel like discussing. Maybe he should call Nancy today and try to smooth things over. Last night seemed like a lousy way to end a relationship that had lasted two years. Two years, for God's sake. One ninth of his life! Shouldn't he expect something more after two years? And if they got back together, wouldn't they just go through the whole scene again at the end of August? Besides, he didn't really feel sad, just out of sorts, as his grandmother used to say. Looking back on it, the whole argument, the whole break-up, felt almost inevitable. He was ready to move on—new school, new friends, new girlfriends— although the thought also left such a knot in his stomach that he threw away what was left of his chicken sandwich.

It was his father who interrupted these reflections. What if the two of them took a drive? An old farmer in the northeastern part of the county had received a foreclosure notice from the bank, and Charles' father agreed to meet with him, take a look at his sheep raising operation. "You're going to be busier starting tomorrow, so I thought maybe we could have this time, just the two of us. The summer will be gone in no time, and then you'll be off at Drake."

Charles agreed, because he was tired of stewing and because he wanted to avoid his mother's questions. But they were barely out of town, headed east on a fairly flat stretch of county road, when his father said, "Your mother tells me you were home early last night. You know how she hears any noise. Everything okay?"

"Yeah, fine."

His father glanced at him, then fumbled for his sunglasses before asking, "So what did you think of worship this morning? I thought the choir was in good form."

"It was okay." They bounced over a rough patch in the pavement before he added, "It was the same as usual. Reverend Shelton just preaches about the same thing. It's always the love of God and how people are basically good, but if they believe God loves them, they can be even better people. Over and over."

"What's wrong with that?"

When Charles didn't answer, his father said, "I saw you talking with Reverend Shelton after worship. Were you discussing the sermon? Sharing great theological insights?"

This ride was a bad idea, Charles thought. But what he said was, "He wants me to stop by for a conversation some day after I get off work, which for some reason he knows is 4:30. He said he's usually around the parsonage or the church that time of day, since he doesn't play golf."

His father smiled. "I've invited him often enough. Playing golf, I've told him, would give him a chance to talk with people in the congregation, maybe even recruit a few new ones."

They drove in silence for a minute until his father said, "Speaking of when you get off work, are you looking forward to working on the street crew?"

"I don't even know what I'll be doing," said Charles. "I don't even know where I'm supposed to go in the morning."

9

"You know very well where it is," said in the authoritative tone Charles hated. "The city garage is just off the square, down that little hill from the café, a hundred feet off the southwest corner," as if precise coordinates were necessary in a town of 2,500.

"Why do they call it the *city* garage, working for the *city*? Lockwood isn't big enough to be called a city."

His father ignored the question. "I know Clyde who heads up the crew, and he will teach you what to do, but he won't put up with any nonsense. He's a tough old bird." When Charles was silent, his father continued. "And then there's Dexter and Moss."

"Moss? Why do they call him that? Doesn't he have a first name?"

"I'm sure he does, but I forget what it is, everybody just calls him Moss. He will tell you—and tell you and tell you—how he was a school teacher in a former life. Now Dexter, he's been there for as long as I can remember. Unlike Moss, he doesn't say much. He must be sixty, though how he's lasted that long smoking his pipe all day I have no idea."

They passed by the dozen or so buildings known collectively as Mason, turning left at the town's Stop sign. "I remember," said his father, "when Clark still ran the Poultry House just east of here. We used to get chickens, eggs, even cream there when I was a kid."

"Yeah, I know, and now the eggs just aren't as good." He could tell, despite the sunglasses, that his father was staring at

10

him. "Well . . . that's what you say every time we come through Mason."

As they drove north, the landscape grew increasingly hilly. They crossed the Fox River, more stream than river; and since it meandered through this side of the county, they crossed it again. As they scaled each hill, the scene beyond came gradually into view, top to bottom: first trees, followed often by a farmhouse, starting with its roof and nearby silo, then fences, animals, and fields. In some places, the land was too hilly for cultivation, and the trees came right down to the road.

They drove in silence, Charles doing his best not to think about Nancy. When that didn't work, he concentrated on the reasons to justify the break-up. But good times kept intruding: rides on his family's boat at Lake Winyan; milkshakes at the Dairy Queen after an evening of studying together; football and basketball games where they cheered side by side; golf as a twosome at the Country Club; the county fair where they sat together in his family's grandstand box; meals with his family (Nancy got along great with his sister, Connie); the sight of her breasts in the back seat of the Buick, and in her living room when the rest of the family was away.

It had all felt . . . comfortable. People at the Country Club told them they belonged together, even looked alike. Vernon, who ran the clubhouse, called them "the clean-cut couple," although Charles had never been sure that was entirely a compliment. They both were thin, but while Charles was

11

reluctant to be seen in a swimming suit, Nancy spent much of the summer perfecting her tan at the town's pool. They both had straight, light brown hair, Nancy's flipped up stylishly above her shoulders, Charles' barely long enough to part. And both had a birthmark on their face, although Nancy's mole near her mouth was called a beauty mark, while the light brown spot near Charles' hairline was sometimes mistaken for dirt. Maybe, he now told himself, he hadn't always been comfortable with Nancy, at least not as comfortable as others thought he was. And, in any case, comfortable can become claustrophobic.

"I bet you've never been down this road," his father said as they turned off the county-maintained pavement and bounced along what was little more than a dirt path. "You could spend years, certainly months, exploring all the corners of this county. Or is that also on your list of things I keep telling you?"

The farmer, a man the age of Charles' late grandfather, met them as they parked on a gravel area near the barn, holding the collar of a barking dog. After the dog was chained to a fence post, the men began their tour of the buildings. Charles trailed behind, occasionally stopping to look across the pasture or peer into the darkened barn, far enough away that he heard only fragments of their conversation: "Worked thirty years at Morrell . . . always wanted to farm . . . only land Ruth and I could afford . . . whose idea was it? . . . have to raise sheep on hills like these . . . then all this polyester and acrylic . . . out of my control . . . cheaper than wool . . . sure it was a bobcat?"

12

Charles stayed outside when the men entered the square, featureless farmhouse. He was about to wander back to the barn when the farmer's wife brought him a glass of iced tea. He was standing by the back stoop, not sure what to do with the glass, when the men pushed open the screen door. "Yeah, Woody was here," the farmer was saying. "Brought the foreclosure notice himself, and not too nice about it. But I guess that's his job. And, then, he's like you . . . said he wanted to see where they found her. That all happened before he became sheriff. Came a second time, too, but I don't really know what for. That's when I called you to see if I got options."

As they were driving back down the bumpy dirt track, Charles asked, "Are you going to help him?"

His father rubbed the back of his neck. "I'm not sure there's much I can do. Mr. Hazelton has a lot of things working against him."

"Did he get himself in this situation?"

"Well, this is his first go at farming, so he's made some mistakes, no doubt about that. But, like he says, there's a lot he can't control."

"What did he mean that the sheriff wanted to see where they found her? Found who?"

"I guess you're too young, although I would have thought you'd have heard about it. When your mother and I came back to Lockwood, right before you were born, a farmer on this property killed his wife. That's what the sheriff claimed, anyway. The

13

farmer claimed she was murdered by a stranger he saw driving off in a pickup. But there didn't seem to be any evidence of this, and it looked like he'd be charged with murder."

"So what happened? Is he still in prison?"

"Well, he never went to prison. Sheriff Andrews, Woody's predecessor, was coming out for one last look around, finishing up his investigation, but the farmer—I can't recall his name right now—apparently thought he was coming to arrest him, so he killed himself. Shot himself right there in the living room, which according to what Hazelton was telling me, is also where the wife died."

"Did they ever find out if he really killed her?"

"Well, that was the end of it."

"So it could have been a stranger?"

His father glanced in Charles' direction. "I suppose. But the sheriff seemed sure. If I'd been his attorney, I would have insisted they dig a little deeper, but the sheriff said he'd investigated enough to know what happened. In any case, the farm went to the couple's kids, who didn't want it. I don't blame 'em. Then a fellow from Illinois bought the farm, but couldn't make a go of it. And that's probably why Hazelton got it cheap. People shy away from places with bad associations. Even Hazelton, who is pretty level-headed, seems to think this place has a dark spirit. I told him that a judge will want other explanations for his troubles."

They were back to the county road, only this time his father turned north rather than retrace their route. "Let's drive through Florence, where we used to go for tenderloins. Remember? Before they closed the café." When Charles didn't respond, his father added, "It's not much farther this way. You'll still be back in plenty of time if you and Nancy have plans for this evening."

"I told Randall I'd hang out with him and Kenny and Cliff," said Charles. And then, because he had to tell someone, "Nancy and I broke up."

His father glanced at him again and nodded. "Well, I'm sorry, but it would have been hard once you were at different schools. Is this final?"

"Yeah . . . I guess so. I should've stuck with Mom's plan for me to work at Drake this summer and stay with Aunt Gloria until school starts."

"Well, too late for that. We're lucky the Copeland kid broke his arm and the spot opened up on this street crew."

"That makes it sound like you're happy Andy broke his arm!"

"I'm just saying you burned your other bridges, like working again in the shoe store. So if this hadn't opened up, and I hadn't heard about it at the city council meeting, I don't know what you'd have been doing. Sweeping the walk and washing a few windows at my office, I guess."

"Or just reading and getting ready for college."

15

"Yes, I know what your mother would prefer, but working some will do you good." They drove for a while, listening to the thump of tires on the asphalt seams, until he added, "But humor your mother and practice the piano."

Randall picked him up that evening a little before sunset. Kenny and Cliff were already in the back seat of the ten-year-old, two-tone Pontiac Chieftain, with its low fins and protruding taillights.

"We left the front seat for you," said Kenny, "since you are the val-e-dic-to-ri-an." They all laughed, including Charles.

"No," said Cliff, "we left it for you so you won't get the back seat all wet cryin' over Nancy."

"Are you gonna call her?" asked Randall. "Things sure happened fast last night. I thought you two were upstairs messing around, and then I heard you'd left. Then we heard you broke up."

Why, Charles wondered, did he suddenly feel so fatigued. "I don't know. I doubt it." He started to ask, *Who told you?* but decided it didn't matter. Instead he said, "I'm not going to meet anybody new riding around with you assholes," which made them laugh and him feel slightly better. "Let's just go."

They sat for a minute in the driveway while Randall turned on the radio and pushed the button for KMOX, so they could listen to the Cardinals. They headed for the Dairy Queen at the north edge of Lockwood, on the highway to Mahaska, but then Charles realized Nancy might be there, so suggested they drive

16

back toward the square, to see who's in town. Randall pulled the Pontiac into a driveway in order to turn around, and then backed out quickly when the porch light came on and a man appeared at the screen door.

He detoured to the east side of town so they could cruise by the high school, now completely dark, then turned toward the square on the road leading in from the Country Club. The courthouse, with its topknot of Lady Justice, loomed in front of them. At that point, Charles decided he actually hoped to see Nancy, show her he was over the relationship or talk to her or something. So they turned back north past the square, where no one seemed to be hanging out, past the home of the local Civil War hero, past the tiny Catholic Church, where Charles had never set foot. But there were mainly families with children at the Dairy Queen. Randall, Cliff, and Kenny each bought a Coke, Charles a root beer float, and then the four of them sat in the car in the parking lot.

"We'll see who shows up," said Cliff. They listened to Harry Caray as the Cardinals took a one-run lead, until Randall said he was worried about running down the car's battery, so they just sat quietly with the radio off.

Randall broke the silence. "So, you're gonna stay for the summer even if you and Nancy—"

"Not much choice."

"And you're still gonna work for the city?"

"Yep."

17

"I can't believe you're gonna work for Clyde!" said Cliff, leaning far over the front seat. "One day, Scott was just standin' on the corner by the old depot, and Clyde drove by in his truck. I was there, saw it myself. I guess he thought Scott was just wastin' time, or somethin' was goin' on. Anyway, he got out of the pickup and beat the shit out of his own kid! Right there on the street!"

"Remember that time," said Randall, "when Frankie came to school with her cheek all swollen? Her eye was practically shut. Remember that? I bet it was Clyde who hit her. Scott wouldn't hit his sister. He was like her bodyguard."

They finished their drinks, and then Randall said, "You're gonna be tired, I can tell you that. You might even get some muscles on those skinny-assed arms!" He grabbed Charles by the bicep and squeezed. "Won't have to wear long-sleeved shirts all the time at Drake." The three of them laughed loudly.

It wasn't that he was unaccustomed to such kidding, and they were by no means the only ones to poke fun at his physique. But this evening, for whatever reason, Charles wasn't in the mood for it. "Why do you say shit like that?" He pushed Randall as he pulled his arm away.

"Well, aren't you touchy," said Randall, still smiling. "Nancy got you so outta sorts you can't even take a joke?"

"Why is the joke always about me? Maybe I'm not Charles Atlas because, unlike you and Kenny, I haven't spent my time dragging hay bales and shoveling pig shit. Maybe I had better things to do." Even as he said it, Charles realized he hadn't meant to sound so angry, or to be so loud.

Randall swiveled to face him, and now he wasn't smiling. "'Maybe I had better things to do,'" this said in a sing-song voice. "Like sit around that fancy house with your piano lessons and your golf lessons."

"So now it's pick on Charles because my parents have a big house. I'm not the one whose parents bought him a car."

Randall continued as if Charles hadn't spoken. "You never even played any sport, did you? Except golf, which doesn't count, riding around in your daddy's cart. What did Nancy think when you took off your shirt, or did you even take it off?" He smirked at his own cleverness, but the other two were silent.

"I played baseball," said Charles, still too loudly. "I was on a Little League . . ." but the whole argument suddenly felt irrelevant, and he stopped mid-sentence. "It doesn't matter." He paused, and no one spoke. "It's not Nancy. Aren't you all sick of this town? This place sucks." Another pause as he glanced over his shoulder at Kenny and Cliff. "I mean, Lockwood's okay, but really—"

They sat in silence, Randall staring straight ahead over the steering wheel of the Chieftain, until Kenny cleared his throat and announced, "I'm going to college."

Charles turned to the back seat. "When did you decide this?" He tried to sound more exuberant. "That's great, man! Where you going?"

19

Kenny looked out the window, not at Charles. "It's not a fancy school in Des Moines, but the community college in Centerville has a program I want."

"That's great. What—"

"Bookkeeping." And then after a pause, "I wasn't valedictorian, was I?"

More silence. Finally, Charles, looking at no one, said, "Sorry I got pissed off, okay? Maybe it's this street crew job my dad has me doing . . . I think I'll just walk home."

After Charles was out of the car, Randall leaned his head out the window. "We'll probably drive around later in the week, if you wanna come with."

"I may be too tired." But that, too, sounded edgy, so he added, "Let's see how things go."

On the walk back, he tried to set his thoughts in order, but they simply wouldn't stay focused.

Chapter Two

Two structures rise above the trees as you approach Lockwood, Iowa—the water tower, with the town's name in large block letters, and the county courthouse. Locals, of course, take the courthouse for granted, but it is so architecturally unusual that outsiders driving through Lockwood often stop to ask how in the world the town ended up with a building that looks like a layer cake with too much frosting. The lower floors are marked by elongated windows, topped with ornamental stone hoods and elaborate cornices. Above this is a sharply sloping roof with protruding ornate windows. Still higher, the building narrows to a bell tower, above which is a heavily-decorated clock, facing four directions—all of it crowned by the statue of blind justice with her sword and scales.

As a child, Charles had called it "the castle," imagining the streets that formed a square around the courthouse as a moat to keep out invaders. This mental image had been enhanced by the stately old trees that dotted the courthouse lawn. But by the time

Charles was in high school, Dutch elm disease had swept through Savannah County like a medieval plague, leaving the courthouse partly exposed and far less imposing. And, in truth, he had only been inside a time or two, when his primary sensation had been how musty it smelled.

Along Highway 52, which touches the southern edge of Lockwood, are signs marking the trail followed by fifteen thousand Mormons in the summer of 1846. Their large herds of cattle, horses, and sheep ate their way through what is now Savannah County on the journey west; but eventually memory of the damage faded, so that even Charles' father, who fancied himself a local historian, had little to say about it.

Highway 19 has no historical markers, but is far more lucrative for Lockwood since it runs through the middle of town, providing speed-trap opportunities for the sheriff and his deputy. On the south side of town, the highway runs past Billy's Auto Parts, with its acres of wrecked cars. Charles' father asked the rhetorical question, *Why does this have to be the first thing people see when they come to Lockwood?!* so many times that Charles could mouth the words with him. The road forms the east side of the square on its way north to Mahaska, exiting the town past the cemetery, which from a distance resembles a crenellated wall on the top of its hill. All of his life, Charles had heard people joke that the only way out of Lockwood is by way of the graveyard.

In many respects, Lockwood is like any small town in southern Iowa. North of the square, on streets named after trees and presidents, are the finer homes, three of them with historical plaques affixed to the front. Just beyond them lies the hospital, conveniently near the cemetery. East of the square, a ways past the high school, is the municipal swimming pool, connected to the little-used city park, and on the edge of town, the Country Club, where much of Lockwood's social life takes place, at least for those who can afford it. West of the square, running along the block where the town keeps piles of sand and gravel, is the train track, at one time Lockwood's reason for being, but now overgrown with weeds. Beyond this are the fairgrounds where, for one week every summer, farm families display their prized baked goods and livestock, and stock cars race precariously around the half-mile track. A midway also appears, complete with Ferris Wheel, Tilt-a-Whirl, and booths for spending money on the off chance of winning a stuffed rabbit or bear.

But it all radiates from the square. Facing the courthouse on all four sides are rows of two-story buildings, many of them dating from a fire that destroyed part of the town in the 1890s. Several businesses on the square were landmarks in Charles' mental landscape: on the north side, the Savannah Bank, Blankenship's Shoes, Fashion on the Square, and beneath his father's law office, Rexall Drugs. The pool hall and Firmin's Insurance lie to the east; Western Auto and Harry's Hardware on the south; and on the west, the creatively-named West Side Café.

23

For young Charles, the square had been a hub of activity, like a bustling market around its castle; but by the time he was out of high school, the square had three vacant storefronts and, even the town's biggest boosters had to admit, a slightly dilapidated feel. Since the café wasn't open for dinner, the west side, which had two of the empty storefronts, felt almost desolate after dark.

There were butterflies in his stomach as Charles got ready for work on Monday morning, although he told himself it was crazy to be anxious about digging holes or painting curbs or whatever he would be doing. He dressed in jeans and a T-shirt, choosing one with sleeves that mostly covered his upper arms. He ate a bowl of cereal and then found on the table by the front door a five dollar bill and a note from his father: "So you can buy some donuts for the boys on the street crew."

Charles picked out a half-dozen doughnuts from Ginny who ran the café, and then walked slowly down the short hill to what he knew must be the place. All he could see from the street were two large sliding doors, but around the corner of the brick building he found a regular door under a faded sign that read "City Garage." He entered promptly at 7:30.

As his eyes adjusted, Charles could see a dump truck and a tractor, with a scoop on one end and backhoe on the other, lined up behind the sliding doors. In the far back corner of the room were tall wooden shelves, on which pieces of equipment were stacked nearly to the high ceiling. In the near corner, three men

24

clustered around a sagging couch and a workbench covered with splotches of paint. On the wall above the workbench was a large pegboard with hanging tools, and next to it an old Frigidaire. Two windows on the back wall were the only natural source of light.

A short muscular man, with a deep tan and a baseball cap pulled low on his forehead, got up slowly from the couch and walked toward Charles. "I'm Clyde. Last time I remember seein' you, you wasn't any taller than that bench." He took Charles firmly by the arm and guided him over to the couch. "This," he said to the other two, "is Robert and Madeleine's boy I told you was comin' to work with us." Charles started to say hello, but Clyde continued. "This here's Dexter," he said gesturing toward a man in overalls who was perched with his legs crossed on the edge of the workbench. Dexter raised his pipe in greeting. "And this fella is Moss," a paunchy, middle-aged man who had been standing by the dump truck and now vigorously shook Charles' hand.

"Clyde said your name is Charles. Do they call you Charlie?" asked Moss.

"I've always gone by Charles, and I—"

"That sounds purdy highfalutin' for a place like this," said Clyde, while Dexter grinned, pipe clenched between teeth, and slapped his knee.

"It sounds," said Moss, "like the name of an English king. I used to teach the whole history—"

25

Clyde spoke over the top of him. "Why don't you stick with Charles at home, and we'll call ya Charlie down here." It didn't sound like a question, so Charles stayed silent while Clyde lit a pipe and handed his pouch to Dexter so he could refill his own. Once it was going, he said, "If your family don't want people callin' you a nickname, they should've called you somethin' like Dexter." Dexter nodded. "Or we could just call ya Weaver, like we call Moss Moss. Sometimes I forget that Moss has a first name." Dexter slapped his knee and Moss managed a faint smile.

Charles realized he was still holding his sack. "I brought some doughnuts, since this is my first day. My dad—"

"Moss's diabetic, or says he is, and Dexter don't eat much sweets 'cause of his teeth, but I'll have one to keep you company." So Clyde and Charles sat on either end of the couch, chewing in silence while the other two watched, Charles feeling increasingly uncomfortable. Should he ask about the work? Should he tell them more about himself? Just as he was ready to do one or the other, Clyde said, "I hear you're goin' to college."

"I went to college," said Moss quickly. "Well, they called it junior college back then, until the money ran out."

"Drake, that what I heard?"

"Yes," said Charles, "I start right after Labor Day."

"That's good." It was the first time Charles had heard Dexter's voice. "That's real good."

26

More silence, Moss fidgeting while the other two smoked, until Clyde took the pipe from his mouth and asked, "What you gonna study?"

"Probably history," said Charles. "I like learning about history, although I don't have to decide for sure my first year."

"That's real good," said Dexter, and perhaps because he was trying to see them, Charles got a glimpse of Dexter's few brown-colored teeth.

"History's good, but I also like literature," said Moss, glancing around to see if he was about to be interrupted. "Especially Shakespeare."

Clyde nodded, his lips pursed. "Yes he does, he surely does." Then, looking at Charles, he asked, "You ever laid cement or put down asphalt?" Charles shook his head. "Ever run a tractor?"

As Charles shook his head, Moss said, "That reminds me of how I was when I started working here, although I'd run a tractor."

"I'm pretty good," said Charles, "with a shovel and a rake. We've got that big yard—" He stopped mid-sentence as Clyde banged his pipe hard against the edge of the couch, knocking ash on the cement floor. "Maybe I'm not the right—"

"From what they tell me," said Clyde, "you're a real fast learner," and Dexter nodded. Clyde checked the large clock over the door where Charles had entered. "Okay, time to get goin'. Charlie, you help Moss fill in where we put some new sewer

27

pipe. Shovel and rake'll come in real handy." He and Dexter smiled in a way that made Charles smile as well. "We'll worry 'bout tractors and all later."

Clyde turned the handle on the garage door in front of the tractor and slid the door up in its track until it was overhead and light flooded in. "You know we work Saturday mornings?" This was news to Charles, although he tried not to show it. "The city council, in its *wisdom*" (he drew out the word) "thinks we need to work some on Saturdays, so we oblige 'em, just not too hard." Dexter grinned and nodded. "Me and Dexter, we usually take Saturdays to clean up the machinery, and do other small stuff that needs doin'. You and Moss'll pick up trash 'round the back of the square. Big stuff they set out in the alley that the garbage boys can't take in their truck. Then you take 'er to the dump."

"I thought we were getting two summer workers," said Moss. Clyde was already part way out the door, but he turned back with a vehemence that caught Charles by surprise. "Goddamn it, Moss! I already told you Flora Hinkle's kid, the basketball player or whatever he played, gets here Thursday. But you're still gonna have to do the Saturday pickup, if that's what you're wonderin' about. These boys ain't here to do all your work for you."

Charles couldn't say the days passed quickly, but they weren't quite as tedious as expected. He and Moss spent Monday filling in the trench, although part way through the task he wondered

28

why they didn't just use the tractor to push the dirt back in. He put this question to Moss who replied, "'Ours is not to reason why, ours is but to do and die.' That's *Charge of the Light Brigade*, which was a real thing." Charles also wondered at Moss' ability to talk nearly non-stop, but since the trench was close to the power station, he couldn't hear most of the monologue.

As the day wore on, he thought about the drive with his father and about the farmer and his wife living in a house where two people had met a violent death. Would he want to live in a house with a past like that? Of course, he wouldn't want to live on a farm at all. For some reason, this led him to think about a conversation the previous week with his sister, Connie. "I bet you don't last a week on the street crew," she had told him. "Because everybody knows you aren't very tough. If they wanted somebody tough, they should've hired a farmer." He did manage to conjugate a few French verbs in his head as he shoveled, and not to think much about Nancy.

Tuesday and Wednesday the four of them worked together, filling in potholes in the paved streets near the hospital. Charles didn't know where Clyde got the load of hot blacktop, which he and Moss shoveled into the holes before Dexter ran over them with the dump truck. Clyde spent the day supervising, which included chiding Moss for not clearing out the holes properly before filling them with new blacktop, and going back and forth to somewhere in the town's badly dented pickup. Since Moss

29

didn't talk as much around Clyde, and Dexter didn't talk much at all, these were quiet days, if you didn't count the roar of the dump truck.

Randall, Cliff, and Kenny picked him up after dinner on Wednesday. No one mentioned Sunday's altercation, although Charles suspected the three of them had discussed it a lot. Randall had managed to swipe two somewhat cold beers from his family's refrigerator, and at first it felt comfortable to cruise the town with these friends, sharing beer and listening to the Cardinals. But by 9:00, Charles just felt weary—and bored. Claiming a headache, he asked them to drop him off.

Their main topic of conversation, along with the hot girls from Mahaska up at Lake Winyan, had been Jerry Hinkle. "I never really talked to him," said Charles. "Just watched him play football and basketball."

"I don't think he talked to anybody except jocks and cheerleaders," said Cliff. "He seemed pretty full of himself around the school. Mr. All-Conference this and All-Conference that." Randall and Kenny acknowledged that they, too, hadn't talked with Jerry Hinkle, since he was a senior when they were sophomores, but they nonetheless agreed with Cliff's overall assessment: "Anybody who's that stuck up will probably be a pain to work with."

So Charles had even more butterflies when he reported for work that Thursday morning. But, in fact, Jerry greeted him like a long-lost friend when they met in the garage, which made him both pleased and relieved, although it was soon clear that Jerry greeted everyone with the confidence of a person who needs no introduction.

Jerry's reception from Clyde was less friendly. His first words were "You goin' swimmin'?"

"It's hot out," said Jerry, smiling broadly. "I know you all don't wear shorts, but you're not against it, are you?"

"There's pro'bly a law 'gainst Moss showin' his legs in public," said Clyde, which made Dexter grin and slap his knee. Clyde stretched while Moss cracked his knuckles and tried to smile. "Well, they're your legs. Wouldn't want mine all scratched up. You may not heard it, but we do real work 'round here."

While Dexter and Clyde smoked in what Charles now thought of as their usual places—one on the end of the workbench, the other on an end of the beat-up couch—Jerry examined the tools hanging on the wall and in the boxes below. Finally, Clyde took the pipe from his mouth and said, "That's a rasp, not some kinda sex toy."

"Who needs a toy?" asked Jerry, and even Clyde smiled.

But it was Dexter who next spoke. "You got a girlfriend?" pointing his pipe not at Jerry, but at Charles. Charles intended to say as little about this as possible, but somehow ended up giving a long-winded explanation of dating Nancy for two years, and how they had just broken up, although he managed to refrain from saying why. He steeled himself for the ribbing, but, after a

31

pause, Clyde said, "College'll be different. 'Round here, people don't appreciate brains, but outside this county the girls'll be knocking on your door. Besides, you don't wanna get tied down to some local girl."

"I heard you were going with her," said Jerry. Really? Jerry Hinkle knew that about him? Charles tried not to show his astonishment, while Jerry added, "Lots of fish in the sea. Maybe we can do a little fishing together this summer." Again Clyde smiled. And again Charles was amazed.

Around 8:00, Clyde gave the daily instructions. He would drive the tractor to what he called the depot, the town's piles of rock and sand. Jerry and Charles would follow in the pickup, and he would put a load of gravel in the back so they could fill in places that needed it in the lanes that crisscrossed the cemetery. Jerry seemed to take for granted that he would drive, but Clyde had other plans. "Let Charlie here get used to that sticky gear shift."

The day was actually enjoyable. When they decided it must be break time, they drove to the Texaco station and bought Cokes in glass bottles from the station's red cooler, then leaned against the pickup parked in the shade, Charles soaking in Jerry's description of college life. Having a car is a real plus, Jerry told him. You can get off campus on weekends, explore the bars in some of the little towns. There is a place on the Mississippi where he liked to take girls for dinner. Sunset reflecting off the river. Very romantic. And there is a motel he liked to use in Davenport.

"What about classes? I mean, how much time do you have to spend . . . studying?"

"I love my courses, most of them," said Jerry. "I like studying people, so . . . who knows? I might end up a psychologist. Or a lawyer, like your dad." Since Jerry was usually smiling, Charles found it hard to tell when he was serious.

When the five of them gathered back at the garage, however, Clyde was in a foul mood and things got testy. It started when Moss asked Jerry if he was playing basketball up there at Iowa State.

"I wouldn't go to Iowa State," Jerry scoffed, with a smile. "That's an ag school."

Clyde's eyes narrowed and he banged his pipe hard on the side of the couch. "'Round here," he said, biting each word, "we happen to think farmers are good people." Jerry started to clarify, but Clyde cut him off. "'Round here, we don't stick our nose in the air when talkin' 'bout good people. If you don't wanna be 'round farmers, maybe you don't wanna be 'round us," this last said with real anger.

"Jesus, I'm sorry!" said Jerry. "I was just—"

Clyde interrupted him. "I hear you was real pissed off when my boy, Scott, was athlete of the year at the high school 'stead of you."

Jerry looked genuinely surprised. "I may have said he only played one sport. That's all I ever said, if I said that."

"Was district wrasslin' champion," said Dexter, while Clyde puffed on his pipe, staring at Jerry.

Jerry shrugged. "Yeah, that's right, he was. So who cares now?"

"You sayin' it don't matter he was champion?"

"No, Clyde, I'm saying it doesn't matter to me whether I was top athlete or not. That was two years ago, for God's sake, and I'm way past that." Then in an obvious effort to change the subject, "Iowa State's a good school, but I go to Iowa. Go Hawkeyes!"

This apparently struck Moss as a good time to rephrase his question. "Do you play basketball at Iowa? Are you practicing this summer?"

"Nah," said Jerry, his normal smile back in place. "I thought I would when I went there, but it didn't seem much fun. There are a million other things to do in college than play basketball, and lots of beautiful women to see about."

With the tension eased, Dexter reported, in one sentence, that he and Moss had graded the old road leading to Lake Corbin, the town's nearby water supply. Moss filled out the report in considerable detail, until Clyde cut him off by asking, "What about you two?"

"We emptied that pile of gravel," said Charles. "Filled in all the holes we could find."

"Though I don't get it," said Jerry. "Isn't there a cemetery board that takes care of that place? Why is it the city's business?" When no one spoke—Charles staring at the floor—he continued. "Just throwing gravel on those roads, paths, whatever they are, doesn't make sense to me either. It'll just get scooped out again when cars drive through there."

"Let me set you straight on somethin'," said Clyde in a voice that at first was barely audible. "In this garage, you don't make decisions, and I don't make *suggestions*," exaggerating the last word disdainfully. "I tell ya to do somethin', ya do it. Or else go home and take care of your mommy." For a minute, the only sound Charles could hear was the ticking of the old clock over the door. Finally Clyde knocked the ash from his pipe and announced that there wasn't enough work for both college boys the next morning. So which one of them would keep Moss company picking up trash around the square, while the other got his beauty sleep and lost four hours pay? After a short silence, Charles said he wouldn't mind working Saturday morning; in fact, he was planning on it, which was fine by Jerry. Dexter removed the pipe from his mouth and nodded.

That evening, however, Charles began to wonder why he had volunteered. He remembered from biology class that there are 650 muscles in the human body, and by the time the family sat down for dinner, he was convinced all 650 of his hurt, and he had only worked one week! His father left the table as soon as the meal was over *to hear what Cronkite has to say about these*

35

Vietnam protests, but Charles simply sat there, trying not to move, while Connie and his mother cleared the dishes and put them in the newly-installed dishwasher.

It was his mother who started the conversation. "You look tired. Why don't you go to bed early so you can get up at a decent hour and maybe go over some French in the morning."

"I'm okay," which he amended to, "I'll be okay. And I work on Saturday mornings. It's part of the job."

"What? Those poor men don't work enough Monday to Friday?"

"Talk to Dad. He's on the city council, and Clyde says it's the council's idea."

His mother clearly had more to say on the subject, but Connie, smiling broadly, jumped in. "I hear your friends are taking bets on whether you last two weeks."

"What are you talking about?! What friends?"

"Randall and those guys you hang out with. He told Becky you'd quit by the first of June."

Now Charles was moving, pushing back his chair and standing up, although he was sorry he'd done it so quickly. "Maybe I should get in on this bet, make some money."

"Oh," said Connie sarcastically, "show them you're a tough guy? Stick it out just because they said you won't? Charles, face it, you're not very tough." She kept the table as a barrier between them, her smile even wider. "You know what else he told

36

Becky? That you'll be back with Nancy by then. But I don't think they're betting on that one since it's a pretty sure thing."

No one was in any hurry to get moving at work on Saturday, which was fine with Charles, but finally around 8:30, he and Moss climbed into the cab of the dump truck, which seemed to Charles even older than the pickup. It was his first time inside the cab, with its jagged tear in the plastic-covered seat and long gear shift column in the middle of the floor. It smelled like grease and plastic and sweat, which, to Charles' surprise, he didn't find overly offensive. Moss fiddled with the choke and pumped the gas pedal until the engine caught, and then gunned the truck loudly up the short hill to the square and into the alley behind the buildings on its south side. In the back of Harry's Hardware, they picked up a couple of boxes filled with smaller boxes and a broken typewriter, things that certainly could have gone on the garbage truck had they been put out in time. There was also a sack of women's clothes from an earlier era.

"I wonder where this came from," said Charles.

Moss peered into the sack and rummaged through the items before declaring, "This would be from Mrs. Thompson."

"But why is it here?"

"Oh, she lives above Harry's in the Wood's old apartment. But that's before your time." Charles decided not to admit that he hadn't known *anyone* lived above the shops on the square, but Moss seemed to intuit it. "Over on the north side, that's where

37

offices like your dad's are. But Mrs. Thompson lives here and Sadie lives above the café, although I don't know how she gets up and down those steps. I think somebody brings food up to her. And two or three people live in the hotel, but none of 'em for very long."

In fact, the Grant Hotel was their next stop. Moss drove the truck, with its fourteen-foot bed, slowly across the two-lane highway, left across another street, and into the alley on the east side of the square. Behind the somewhat shabby hotel, where Charles had never set foot, was an old metal desk and a wooden swivel chair, badly scratched and missing two of its casters. Moss studied both pieces carefully, twisting his neck until it popped and cracking his knuckles. At last he said, "We need to take these to Dexter's."

"Dexter needs a desk?"

"Not for his house here," said Moss. "It wouldn't fit in his house here. That house's not big enough to swing a cat in. It's to save it for his place on the Lake of the Ozarks."

"Dexter has a house on the Lake of the Ozarks?!"

"You should ask him about it," said Moss. "He doesn't have a house there yet, but somebody—an uncle or some relative, I forget—gave him a piece of land somewhere on the lake, or near the lake, one of the lakes; so if we find good furniture, we take it to him for the house he's going to build, and he keeps it in his backyard. We got a davenport one time from behind the insurance office. Nice green color. And," he smiled, "there was a

38

really fine chair, just one tear in the fabric, that I bet your dad put out from up in his office. I would've taken it, but it'll look fine in Dexter's house. I told him he should put it in his house here, but he says he wants to save it for his house in the Ozarks."

They lowered the tailgate and wrestled the desk and swivel chair onto the back of the truck, Moss wedging the boxes against the upside down chair to keep it from sliding. After they finished the east side of the square, Moss left the alley and headed back south, stopping in front of a small, plain house, four blocks off the square on a gravel-surfaced street. The house had a white metal canopy, smudged with dirt and badly dented, over the cement stoop in the front, where, according to Moss, Dexter sat most evenings listening to the Cardinals. A chainlink fence enclosed the backyard in which Moss and Charles deposited the furniture next to a tarp-covered pile.

"Dexter can take it from here," said Moss. "I bet he'll be happy with this desk, because I know he doesn't have one yet for his house." He smiled from under his cap that looked a size too small. "I'll tell him you found it."

As they returned to the square and completed their tour of the alleys, Moss kept up a steady patter, which Charles found he actually enjoyed. He learned that Dexter is married, although Moss hasn't seen his wife more than a time or two since her health isn't good. Maybe something to do with her heart, although he wasn't sure. Dexter had moved to Lockwood from somewhere in Arkansas when he got married, because his wife is from Savannah County, but Moss couldn't remember when or how they met. Charles also learned that Clyde had grown up, not on an Iowa farm, but on a Wyoming ranch where his father raised horses. "You see how bow-legged he is?" Clyde had been in World War II, Moss was sure of that, but he couldn't remember if he was an officer. "If he wasn't," said Moss, "he should've been."

Finally, as they headed slowly out of town—past the Dairy Queen, then past the cemetery—on the highway to Mahaska, Charles asked Moss about himself. "Were you born in Lockwood?"

"In Mahaska," said Moss, "because Lockwood didn't have a hospital in those days, though a lot of people didn't use a hospital to have a baby anyway." He shifted, with difficulty, into fourth gear and looked at Charles. "I was in high school with your dad." He tilted his head back until his neck popped. "I always wanted to be a teacher. I *was* a teacher—seventeen years in the country school out by Stiles." He sucked in his cheeks while breathing deeply, and when he spoke again, it was in a different tone. "We had a good school. At one time, before my time, it went through eighth grade. Kids came from the farms all around that part of the county. It was a good school! But now all the money goes to the towns, for their schools with their fancy football fields and whatnot. So they close down schools like mine. Consolidating they call it."

After a pause that felt to him increasingly awkward, Charles asked, "Did you teach after that in Lockwood?"

Moss cracked his knuckles on the steering wheel. "Oh, they wanted a college degree by then. Said my experience was good, and all that, but . . . that's water under the bridge." He sucked in his cheeks, and then said, in a voice so low that Charles could barely hear over the roar of the truck, "I told them about teaching *Julius Caesar*—you know, the play—I love that play, and somehow they got the idea I didn't know he was real. Told me that's why I needed more than a year of junior college . . . where I was a good student . . . really was . . ." his voice trailing off.

"Why did they think that?"

Moss breathed deeply and shook his head. "I said something about how good Shakespeare was at making things up, which he was, but I guess they got the wrong impression."

"Couldn't you clear that up? You know, tell them they misunderstood you." But the words sounded false to Charles as soon as he said them, and Moss just shrugged.

They turned east down a pitted gravel road that was as new to Charles as the back side of the square. He watched as Moss, the sleeves of his tan work shirt rolled up to the elbows, shifted down to third. "Anyway," said Moss, "I got this job, which pays enough so I could help Calpurnia go to beautician school. It's not college, but, hey, now she's got a job over in Fairfield, and even a boyfriend who seems like he's nice to her."

It was as if a puzzle piece slid into place. Charles knew Callie Moss. Well, sort of knew her, because she was leaving high school as he was beginning; but still, why hadn't he put two and two together. Moss wasn't just . . . Moss. He was the father of someone he knew.

They jolted over the road that was untouched by a road grader, past houses that seemed to rest flat on the ground, and then past two trailers, weeds forming a green fringe around them. Was it only a week ago that he was on his way to Missouri to buy condoms?

"It's funny," said Moss, "I've been at this job almost as long as I was a teacher. I guess that means I shouldn't say I'm a teacher, should I? Just a guy on the street crew."

Charles could smell the dump, what his father referred to as the Savannah County Landfill, before he could see it. Moss shifted down to second gear in order to make a sharp turn, and there it was, spread across the site of an abandoned strip mine, some of the garbage piled twenty feet high. They quickly unloaded the boxes and Mrs. Thompson's sack of clothes, and were getting back in the truck, when they heard two gun shots—close by. Moss climbed down from the cab and walked toward a boy who was holding an old hunting rifle. Charles followed at a distance, but close enough to hear Moss ask, "Aren't you Wilson's kid?" The boy nodded almost imperceptibly. "You practicing for deer season?"

"Nah," said the boy, "just shootin' rats."

The boy wandered off, but Moss stayed put, and Charles saw that the older man was staring, not at the piles of garbage, but at a hawk that floated over a nearby field. They stood together until the bird was out of sight, sharing the moment without saying a word. As they hoisted themselves back into the dump truck, Charles experienced that warm, tingling sensation that comes when you feel relaxed, comfortable. No thought of Drake or books or piano, just being there with nothing to do but ride and look and listen.

"After I stopped teaching—after they stopped me teaching—I was with the garbage boys for a month or two," Moss said as the truck roared to life. "But then Leroy Huggins had his heart attack, and a spot opened up on the street crew. Sometimes I think Clyde still thinks of me as the guy from the garbage truck." They bounced back to the highway and headed slowly for town, Moss less concerned with driving than with talking about how the kid with the rifle could amount to something if he just got an education. The kid needs to get it through his head that the world is bigger than Savannah County, Moss was saying, when he looked in the rearview mirror and stiffened, breathing in sharply. Charles glanced over his shoulder and saw the revolving light.

Moss popped his neck and looked ashen as the man Charles knew to be the county sheriff made his way slowly to the side of the truck. "I knew it had to be you, Moss, before I even looked inside. Except I see now you got an accomplice."

"Hi Woody," said Moss softly.

43

"That's Sheriff Wood to you, Moss!" His voice wasn't soft, and he hit the truck's door hard with something in his hand that Charles couldn't see. "You on some sort of excursion, Moss? Goin' slow so you can take in all the scenery?"

"We're coming from the dump. Every Saturday—"

"The dump. Well, that sure explains it. A person has to go real slow on the highway when they're comin' from the dump." He laughed, without humor. "You know how fast you were goin'?"

Moss shook his head and popped his neck. "The speedometer on this truck," he said softly, "doesn't really work."

"Well, I'll tell you," said the sheriff, not softly. "You were going slow enough to impede traffic. That's what the law says: it is against the law to drive on a highway so slow that you impede the normal flow of traffic."

"But there wasn't—" The sheriff cut him off.

"What does this tell me, Moss? I'll tell you what it tells me. It tells me you're the same lazy son of a bitch you've always been. Just like you, drive so slow you won't have to do any more work. A real good model, don't you think, for the Weaver kid," nodding toward Charles.

Moss was twisting his neck, but it wouldn't pop. He cracked his knuckles on the wheel, while the sheriff walked to the front of the truck, where Charles could see he was carrying an oversized flashlight, and then back. "I think this time, Moss, I'll give you a ticket. See if that lights a fire under you. Or maybe

44

they'll just fire ya. Yeah, maybe I'll just tell Clyde I found you drivin' so slow you were a hazard to the real drivers on my highway."

Moss drew a deep breath in through his nose, and Charles wondered if his friend (wasn't he his friend?) was about to cry. He wanted to say something, to tell the sheriff that having a terrible truck wasn't Moss' fault, or that Clyde had encouraged them to take it easy, but that didn't seem like it would be good for Clyde. While he tried to sort this out, the sheriff laughed again. "Yeah, maybe that's what I'll do," he said as he headed back to the patrol car.

They drove the rest of the way to the garage in silence. Charles had planned to get in nine holes of golf that afternoon, but after three holes found he had no enthusiasm for it, and spent the rest of the day trying to read in his room.

Chapter Three

Charles, the budding historian, had once interviewed his grandfather for a school project, one of the many he had done either because they were assigned or for extra credit. He had scribbled furiously on one of his father's yellow legal pads while his grandfather reminisced, sitting on the porch of his grandparents' house just east of the square.

Weavers, his grandfather reminded him, have long been part of Savannah County. His own grandparents had moved here not long after Iowa became a state in 1846. Bought a small farm north of Lockwood when land was practically being given away. His father continued to farm that land—corn, soybeans, a vegetable garden, a few pigs and chickens—and he had been born right there in the farmhouse, in the room his father had added on, just before the turn of the century. And his sister, Vera, Charles' great aunt, had been born in that same room a few years after.

This much Charles already knew (his father never missed an opportunity to extol the family's roots in Savannah soil), but he had other questions for his grandfather, like: why hadn't he stayed on the farm? Well, it just wasn't big enough to provide a good living. So, when a neighbor offered to buy it, the family agreed. They hated to sell—there is something about having land that gets in your blood—but it allowed him to go to junior college and have a good career selling farm equipment. That opened the door for Charles' father to go all the way through law school. And who knows how far Charles can go.

"It looks like you're gonna be tall, like your dad. And you always were a smart kid, same as him, like the time you won the spelling bee for the county."

"Actually, Grandpa, I won it several times."

"And I remember—was it two years ago?—when you went to Des Moines to be part of a pretend Congress."

"The Model UN."

"Yes, that's right. Everybody knows you'll go far, but this will always be where you're from: Lockwood, Savannah County, Southern Iowa."

Then the question at the heart of the school project: what big changes has he seen in his lifetime? Oh, my! Where to begin? When he was a boy, the family still traveled by horse and wagon, and one time on the train all the way to St. Louis. Now you can fly across oceans. All in his lifetime! They used an outhouse all of his growing up years, and their part of the county didn't have

48

electricity until Roosevelt got that program started in the 1930s. Kerosene lanterns, woodstoves, washboards. Think about that compared to the house Charles lives in with all its machines and gadgets. Then there are movies and television and x-rays and penicillin and vaccines. All in his lifetime!

Of course, not all of the changes have been so positive, his grandfather acknowledged. The big farms have gotten richer, while the others struggle to make it, although maybe that's just the way of the world. Cities seem to have gotten worse, with all the riots and pollution. Has Charles heard about the smog in Los Angeles? And there certainly weren't nuclear weapons, and all this other high-powered military stuff they are using in Vietnam, when he was growing up. But he wasn't one of those who wanted things to stay the same, that's for sure. Charles and his generation have a lot to look forward to.

The interview was unfortunately abbreviated because of a piano lesson, something Charles regretted all the more when his grandparents were killed less than a year later in a collision with a semi on the road to Keosauqua. His father railed about how that stretch of highway still has a curb, which, he was sure, contributed to the crash. In the end, however, there was nothing even a lawyer could do but bury them and mourn. And put flowers on their grave, which the family did on that Memorial Day—Monday, May 29—the beginning of Charles' second week of work on the street crew.

The plot was marked by a large granite stone with the name WEAVER chiseled on it, and had space for Charles' father and mother. Charles had read that some people don't care where their body is buried. After all, by that point you're just dead. But in Lockwood, it seemed to console the living to know their clan was collected around a big headstone bearing the family name. Charles took the wisdom of that for granted, although he had once heard his mother say that she'd already spent enough time in Lockwood. She didn't need to spend eternity there, too.

On Tuesday, his muscles hurting far less than the previous week, Charles met his father for a round of golf after work. This meant riding in his father's golf cart, with its striped yellow canopy, which he didn't much like; but it seemed like a good place, away from possible family interruptions, for the conversation he had been mentally rehearsing.

As they rode down the second fairway, Charles recounted the scene with Moss and the sheriff in passionate detail. "He was just being a bully! He didn't even give Moss a ticket, just toyed with him to make him feel bad!"

"Well, Woody can be like that, all right," said his father. "I remember one time he got suspended for making Earl Short, who *was* short, take off his pants, and then he put them up a tree." His father smiled, but then quickly suppressed it. "Mainly, though, he just tried to be the jokester, especially with bigger kids."

"So you were in high school with him, too?" His father took a sip of his Coke and put the cup back in its holder. They had reached Charles' ball, but neither of them got out of the cart.

"It sounds like Moss told you we were in school together. Well, yes, all three of us were there at the same time. Moss was easy to pick on, and, as I remember, Woody picked on him even then." He smiled. "Funny how people can start in the same place, end up in the same place, but really be in such different places."

Charles wasn't smiling. "I don't get it. If people know what he's like, why do they keep electing him sheriff? Did you vote for him?"

"Oh, quit acting so indignant! Electing someone sheriff doesn't mean you'd invite him over for dinner." It was the tone Charles hated, a tone designed, he knew from experience, to shut off discussion. But he continued to stare at the older man, until his father said, "Woody keeps the county pretty safe, especially compared to places where they've started making drugs out on the abandoned farms. We don't need that here, and all that goes with it." As Charles got out of the cart, his father added, "We had a policeman; you may remember him. He was a disaster! Always drinking beer in the Legion Hall. And that makes Woody all the more popular around Lockwood. He's what we've got. We'll all be glad we have Woody, you included, if something really bad ever happens around here."

"I just hope he doesn't say anything to Clyde."

51

"Oh, he won't," said his father quickly. "Woody's afraid of Clyde, because Clyde won't take any of his nonsense. He'll tell him, in no uncertain terms, to stop bothering his workers. Clyde protects his own. You don't have to worry about that."

After the sixth hole, Charles told his father he was stopping, claiming fatigue. The response was predictable. As he walked toward the clubhouse, golf bag over his shoulder, he could hear his father yell, "Connie's right. You *do* need to toughen up."

Charles and Jerry spent the week repainting the faded yellow curbs around the square and stenciling "No Parking" in various places around the hospital and high school. On Monday, they squatted awkwardly in front of the curbs. Charles could also kneel, if he cleared away any rocks, but that didn't work for Jerry in his shorts. So on Tuesday, they took two old dollies from the garage and, with paint cans between their legs, rolled along the curbs. People stopped to joke about their unusual painting technique, and to wonder what Clyde thought about it. "I wouldn't let him catch me doing that if I was you boys," said one old man. "You know what he thinks about people sitting down on the job." In fact, Clyde did drive by around noon in his own pickup. He briefly surveyed their progress, asked Jerry, who was still wearing shorts, if he'd mistaken the dolly for one of them goddamn surfboards, and drove off without further comment.

Later in the week, Charles tipped over a paint can while moving the form they used to stencil "No Parking," leaving a sizable yellow blob on the cement. He and Jerry debated whether to say anything about it when they returned to the garage, since they had soaked up most of the spilled paint with rags a handyman at the hospital had given them; but as they gathered that afternoon around the couch and workbench, Charles found himself telling Clyde what had happened. Clyde stared at his pipe and looked as if he was about to say something, but then waved his hand dismissively. "I bet," he said, pointing his pipe at Charles, "you don't set a can near that form again."

The following Monday, Clyde and Dexter were in their usual places, but spread out on the workbench were two pairs of heavy coveralls covered in black splotches, like an abstract expressionist painting. "Today," said Clyde, "we'll oil them streets out west by the fairgrounds. People already complainin' 'bout the dust, and it ain't even the middle of June." He beckoned Charles and Jerry to follow him into the alley behind the garage, where there sat a small tanker truck, emitting waves of heat. "We get it for a couple a days ever' so often from the state highway fellas," he told them. "Works pretty darn good for an old one."

Charles had never paid much attention to the streets near the fairgrounds, but as he, Moss, and Jerry drove there in the pickup, he saw they were lined with houses that, to him, all looked pretty much like Dexter's: small, one-story, several with vegetable gardens on the side or in the back. Moss seemed to follow his gaze. "This place," he pointed out the passenger side window,

53

"used to belong to old man Simmons. He died there in his rocking chair on the screened-in porch, and now that Italian family lives there. Nice people. This house on the corner nearly burned down a couple of summers ago, but people around here got their hoses and buckets and put it out. See this place with the big porch and those old cars out back? That's where Billy's son, Jake, lives. You know, Billy's Auto Parts. The kid could have the business handed to him if he'd straighten up and fly right. He's got a nice enough house, though."

Once the other two arrived in the tanker, Dexter and Moss put on their gear: the heavy coveralls that slipped inside tall, rubber boots; heavy work gloves that overlapped the sleeves, tied at the wrist with twine to make sure no skin was showing; an old, floppy hat; a kerchief covering their nose and mouth, and goggles. Charles was reminded first of astronauts, and then of his sun- and insect-phobic mother preparing for a day at the lake, which made him laugh, leading Moss to declare in a muffled voice that there was nothing funny about being inside such an outfit.

Clyde, of course, drove the tanker. Once he left the pavement and started down a dirt and crushed-rock street, Dexter and Moss pulled the levers that released a spray of thick, heated oil, covering not only the roadway but the plants alongside. Clyde had chosen this day because there wasn't supposed to be much wind, but little globs of the tar-like spray still ended up all over the men riding on the tanker's back ledge.

After they had covered five or six blocks—the smell of oil nearly overpowering—Dexter and Clyde took off in the pickup and returned with the dump truck, which they had filled with sand on Saturday while Charles and Moss were making their garbage run. Hooked on top of the tailgate was a funnel-shaped machine, its long spout ending above a metal disk. "That sand spreader," Moss told his young audience, "weighs more than a good-sized man. A lot more. Seems impossible, but I've seen Clyde lift it up by himself. 'What a piece of work is a man,'" he quoted, gesturing with both hands, "'noble in reason, something something something in strength.'"

"Okay," said Clyde, as they all stood under a large maple tree, drinking water from the city thermos, "now it's you boys' turn to do some work." So Charles and Jerry climbed into the back of the truck where two shovels were sticking up from the dune. As Clyde drove down the oil-covered streets—slow at first, then faster—the two of them shoveled sand into the funnel, until sand covered oil as oil covered dirt.

It was impossible to talk while keeping the funnel filled with sand, so Charles let his imagination run. He could picture himself at Drake, recounting his summer work exploits to some young co-ed who, in his mind's eye, didn't look a thing like Nancy. The recounting would be even more dramatic if he were on the back of the sprayer, but throwing sand made the point: there was more to him than just his brain.

55

By 4:00, when even Jerry was clearly exhausted, Clyde pronounced them done for the day. Then, as the five of them slumped on the couch or leaned on the workbench, he let them know one more day should do it. "The people in that neighborhood don't want us around any longer than that," said Moss, and for once, Clyde agreed with him.

The next day, however, started contentiously. Moss informed everyone that his diabetes was acting up. And besides that, the smell of oil had affected his sinus condition to the point that he could hardly breathe. For a long minute, Clyde said nothing, smoking his pipe while he stood by the workbench, staring out one of the small back windows. But when he turned, it was so fast that Charles hardly saw him do it, or saw him slam the stick he was holding on the bench so hard it shattered in several pieces. "I got an idea, Moss. Why don't you just take your Shakespeare-quotin' ass outta here for good!"

Charles could hear Moss' neck crack, and then his knuckles. "I do a lot of hard work, Clyde. You know that if I was feeling better —"

"Even when you work, you ain't worth a goddamn. We got this goddamn tanker for a day, and you—"

"I'll do it," said Charles. Everyone turned in his direction, but when no one spoke, he added, "Really. I can ride on the back of the tanker. Just throw the lever, right? And shut it off at the right time."

Clyde puckered his lips in what Charles hoped was a slight smile. "You still have to shovel sand. Moss sure as hell ain't gonna do it in his *delicate condition.*"

"Yeah, that's okay."

Clyde nodded and took his time knocking the ash from his pipe on the side of the couch. "Well, I guess a man ain't a man 'til he sticks the tractor and gets oil all over him. Ain't that right, Dexter?" Dexter nodded, rocking back and forth, legs crossed, on the edge of the workbench.

So it was Charles who donned the space suit, which was much hotter than he had imagined, heat intensified by the heated oil, so thick that it practically bounced on the dusty, rocky streets, watching Dexter intently to make sure he pushed the levers the instant the sprayers crossed the beginning or end of a street. Then off with the space suit, his shirt and pants drenched with sweat, and up into the dune where the sand stuck to him like breading on fried catfish.

Back in the garage, every muscle hurting, Charles discovered that sometime during the day Clyde had stashed beer in the old refrigerator. "We gotta celebrate," he told them. "Charlie's first day as an oilman." Moss said to no one in particular that, as a diabetic, he shouldn't drink beer unless he also had something to eat, at which point Clyde said that didn't matter because he wasn't offering *him* any. But the tension was immediately defused by the arrival of the three-man garbage crew, there at Clyde's invitation.

57

To Charles' astonishment, it was Dexter who told them about the day, starting with how Charles got so covered in oil he almost slipped off the ledge of the tanker. "An' then these boys get to shovelin' sand. Clyde's drivin', goin' 'bout ten. I says, 'you sure makin' them boys work today,' an' he says, 'watch this.' He shoves 'er in second, and you never seen nobody shovel like them two!" Dexter slapped his knee, and the garbage men laughed loudly. "An' then Clyde, he leans out the winder an' hollers, 'I got to speed 'er up a bit,' an' then the sand, she was really a flyin'!" More knee slapping.

"You mean to tell me," said Chuck, the burliest of the garbage crew, "that this skinny-looking kid with my name is actually doing some work?"

"That's what he's tellin' ya," said Clyde. "I'm thinking of makin' Moss take up golf so he can get in shape like Charlie here." And everyone laughed again, even Moss.

Chuck finished his beer and set the bottle on the workbench. "How many streets you got to oil?" he asked.

Clyde shrugged. "Just wait for enough of 'em to complain before we do it."

"Then how do you know how much money you'll need from the city or how many times you need to borrow that tanker?"

Clyde shrugged again, and it was Charles who finally spoke. "Why don't Jerry and I do a survey? Somebody did a survey in 1920-something when there were thirty-two miles of cement sidewalks and five miles of paved streets. So we should be able

58

to do one today, no sweat. Find out how many might need to be oiled."

The others stared at him—Jerry with a big smile, Chuck with raised eyebrows—before Clyde said, "How the hell you know that?"

"It's in an old history of Lockwood. I remember it from a report I did for school."

Chuck looked at Clyde and raised his arms. "Well, for once, you may've got some summer help that's not more trouble than it's worth," and Dexter slapped his knee.

Charles had planned to meet Randall and the others after dinner, but as they were leaving the garage, Jerry said, "Why don't we drive to a bar I like in Missoura, have something to eat and a few beers," and Charles immediately said yes.

Jerry picked him up in his red Camaro z28, with its two wide black stripes on the hood. Charles was surprised when Jerry took the Stringville Road, and even more so when he saw their destination was Don's Café and Tavern, across the intersection from the source of his unused condoms. "Woody likes to patrol the roads out of Missoura," Jerry explained. "Likes to stick it to people under twenty-one who have to cross the border to have a legal drink. But he doesn't pay much attention to this old road, in case I have a beer too many."

It turned out, however, that the real reason for going to Don's was a waitress named Sandy. After they were seated, he told Charles, "I met her a couple of weeks ago, and we've been getting it on." He raised his eyebrows suggestively.

"Really?! You haven't been home much longer than that. How'd you meet her?"

"She's the friend of a friend." He waved, but Sandy was still busy with another customer and didn't look up.

"So you met her a couple weeks ago, and you mean you're having sex with her?" It was more a statement than a question.

Jerry looked away from Sandy and back to Charles. "Sure. Why not? I want to. She wants to." He gestured in Sandy's direction. "Look at her. She doesn't think so, but I think she has a great body. She tells me she was almost a cheerleader in Lancaster." He leaned across the table, with its napkin dispenser and glass salt and pepper shakers. "Last week, she bought a big package of different colored panties, and says she wants me to be sure to see the whole set," said with a confidence that left Charles shaking his head.

"When do you meet her?"

"She usually gets off here at 9:00, and then we go park somewhere. Although I need to figure out something better, because she thrashes around and that doesn't work so well in my car."

Charles looked down at the table and again shook his head. "Well . . . I'm in the way then."

"No, no. I told her you might come with me sometimes. We can just drive back to Lockwood and drop you off. No problem.

That is, if she's even free. I think she said something about her sister coming into town from somewhere."

It looked as if Sandy was ready to head their way, so Charles asked quickly, "Do you do it with girls from Lockwood?"

"When I was there in high school," said Jerry. "I screwed around with some of the girls in my class. Nobody younger, though. I don't go in for that."

Sandy arrived to take their order, and Jerry introduced them. "I'm glad to finally meet you," she said with a big smile. "Jerry talks about you a lot, and my friend from Lockwood says you're really smart." Once again, Charles was amazed. Not only because Jerry talked about him, but because she was so . . . nice. How did Jerry know she wasn't another Nancy? Of course, maybe she would be another Nancy with him. Maybe Nancy would be a Sandy with Jerry.

When Sandy had gone, Charles really wanted to talk about this, but he also didn't want to sound too naive, so instead, after Jerry put a dime in the wall-mounted jukebox, he asked, "Why did you come back to Lockwood for the summer, anyway?"

"You know. I told you. My mom's been sick."

"But why the street crew?"

Jerry smiled. "Why not? It's outdoors. Good exercise. Get a tan. Let's me do what I want in the evenings." Sandy set two beers on their table, and when she left again, Jerry took a big gulp of his and asked, "Why'd you want to know that?"

"I just thought, like Moss said, that you would be at some basketball camp, getting ready for one season or another."

And for the first time since Charles started working with him, Jerry seemed angry. "I wish people would stop telling me what they think I ought to be doing! That's who I used to be— Jerry Hinkle, basketball player—all right? People in Lockwood want me to stay a kid, to be somebody they remember. That's why I don't hang out there much." He took another long drink of his beer, then leaned across the table, smile back in place, and punched Charles in the shoulder. "That's one reason I like you, Charles. You don't act like a jock, or expect me to act like one. Neither do the guys on the street crew, for the most part." He laughed. "Clyde doesn't even think of me as a jock because I didn't wrestle."

Jerry went to the restroom, and while he was up spoke to Sandy who confirmed that she would be with her sister, who (he checked on Charles' behalf) is married. "That's okay," he told Charles. "Aren't you tired, shoveling all that sand? I'm totally beat. I need to go home and get some sleep." So, after eating a hamburger and fries at the table, they moved to the bar for two more beers, and then headed back up the Stringville Road.

Charles later remembered seeing the light of the nearly-full moon on the hedge rows. What animals, he wondered, were hidden in those thin strips of trees and bushes that ran along the edge of the fields? He remembered that something by The Doors was playing on Jerry's eight-track tape deck, remembered feeling the familiar tingle in his stomach as Jerry sped over the tickly hills, bouncing on the asphalt patches, remembered Jerry swerving to miss the still-bloody carcass of a raccoon or opossum. They zipped past the overgrown foundations of what was once Stringville, past the Clyman place, past the pond where he had gone fishing, past the partially-collapsed barn, its angles made sharper by the moonlight. And he remembered hearing the sound of loose gravel as the powerful car slid and tilted until, clutching at the dashboard, he knew they were in the drainage ditch, and he could see the round end of a culvert rushing toward them—when the car jerked left, and somehow they were back on the pavement.

Jerry slowed the Camaro and pulled into a dirt turnoff blocked by a gate, where they sat for a minute in silence. Finally, Charles took a deep breath and asked, "What happened? Did you fall asleep?"

"Maybe, for a second. Oh, man! We were in the ditch, all the way down in the ditch. I'm glad something told me to gun it." He leaned back in the driver's seat and stretched. "I guess all's well that ends well."

Charles took another deep breath and realized his hands were still shaking. "What if there'd been a stump or a big rock in that part of the ditch? Or if you hadn't been able to get control?"

"Or if I had a different car."

More silence. "I keep thinking—" Charles started to say.

63

Jerry finished the sentence: "—of your grandparents. I get it. I saw their car, all smashed up, when they towed it to Billy's."

"Yeah, but also I was thinking of Jimmy Branch. You remember him? He was in my class, or at least he was for a while." Jerry nodded. "One minute he's fine, dives in that creek, hits his head, and he's paralyzed for life. One minute! One stupid, screwed-up decision."

"I get it," said Jerry, as he backed the car slowly onto the road and pointed it north toward Lockwood.

Clyde, of course, would never say, "Take it easy," but the day after their sand shoveling, he instructed Charles and Jerry to touch up a few curbs, and even helped them load the dollies into the bed of the pickup. As they rolled slowly along, looking for places to perfect, they avoided, as if by mutual agreement, talking directly about the near accident. Jerry did report that he had checked the undercarriage, and it looked okay as far as he could tell. When Charles stayed silent, he added that he was going to wash the car after work to get the mud off. Then he added that Sandy was probably still with her sister, and, besides that, he just didn't feel like driving to Missoura every evening. "We don't need to go there to drink beer," he assured Charles, taking it for granted that Charles was with him. "I've got a friend here who'll buy for us."

"Yeah, that's good," said Charles. "Why go to Missoura?" Then, after a pause, "What if we take it over to Dexter's, have a beer with him on his stoop?"

Jerry's smile grew wider, as he nodded. "Sure. Why not?"

Jerry picked him up around 7:30, and, with Charles directing, drove the freshly-washed Camaro to the gravel street south of the square. When Charles announced that Dexter's house was just down the block, Jerry parked the car. "Let's walk to his place from here."

Dexter was out front on the six-foot-square slab of concrete that protruded from his house, sitting in a green and white folding lawn chair, with part of the webbing hanging from the seat. He wasn't wearing his cap, and the line where it normally sat made his head look two-tone. Beside the chair and next to a pile of ash was a small transistor radio, from which came the familiar voices of Harry Caray and Jack Buck. Surprisingly, at least to Charles, Dexter didn't seem surprised to see them. When Charles asked, "Can we listen with you?" he said, "I reckon so," and pointed with his pipe to the edge of the stoop, where they sat after he handed them each a beer.

They listened as Mike Shannon made an error that cost the Cardinals a run. "He's an outfielder," said Dexter. "Ain't no damn good at third base. Need to do what you're good at." But it was cursing at someone with whom you are intimate.

They listened quietly to another inning. Finally, Jerry asked, "Have you ever seen the Cardinals play—you know, in person?"

Ten seconds. Fifteen seconds. "Too many people for me," Dexter finally said. "I can hear 'em right here, I reckon." He puffed on his pipe. "But I seen you play."

"I don't remember seeing you at any of my games," said Jerry.

Another puff. "I mean both of ya."

Charles was astonished. "I only played in Little League one year, as a sub."

"I seen ya." Two puffs. "You done okay. Just a little scrawny back then."

They sat listening to the game, Charles trying to formulate the right question, but it was Jerry who asked, "You have children, Dexter?"

Ten seconds. "The wife's too sickly." A puff. "My brother, he's got a passel . . . down in Arkansas."

"Moss told me," said Charles, "that you have property in Arkansas on the Lake of the Ozarks."

Now it was Jerry's turn to be astonished. "Is that true?"

Dexter nodded as he puffed. "On one of them lakes. Near it, anyways."

"You have a house there?"

Two more puffs. "Gonna build me and the missus a cabin."

"With a front porch," said Charles.

They all smiled, and Dexter nodded. "Yep, with a porch."

That Saturday, there was a party at the Country Club to celebrate the recent high school graduates, or at least those whose parents were members of the Country Club. Charles wasn't wild about going, which he knew was also true of his mother; but, as his father reminded him, many of the Club members were good friends of the family and had supported him over the years. The Club's board had even voted to give him a small college scholarship. "They believe in you. They know you're going to go places," his father told him.

Charles initially clustered with his friends, including Jack and Stephanie, although this was awkward since Nancy was there but wouldn't join them. So when his father urged—told—them to mix with the older generations, Charles was happy to comply.

The first conversation he joined, or at least observed, was about whether to thin out the trees along the stream that bordered the golf course. As it got more heated, voices raised, he floated to a second group just in time to hear one of the town's doctors say, "It's going to be a big problem in this county, no doubt about it. We've already seen a handful of overdose cases in the hospital."

"I've read," said one of his parent's bridge partners, "that they can stir it up at home out of cold medicine and things we use 'round here for fertilizer."

"It could be a real plague before long," said the doctor. "The stuff can be explosive, and you can smell it a mile away. That's

67

why it's taking hold in counties like ours, out-of-the-way places where even the Woodys of the world can't find who's doing it."

"Not much goes on around here Woody doesn't know about," said another friend of the family, and the adults all laughed. He turned to Charles. "At least we don't have to worry about Charles and his buddies getting mixed up in drugs."

"This *is* a big problem," said the manager of the local bank, "but it's not the biggest one we've got." Three of the men took this as a cue to gulp their cocktails, while he continued. "You probably heard, Hancock just sold his farm to a company out of Kansas City. Say they're gonna raise two thousand, maybe three thousand, hogs on that one farm. Unless Jacobs sells, then they'll put those farms together and raise more."

"I wouldn't wanna live downwind of that," said the bridge partner. And while a couple of the men smiled, no one laughed.

"I thought Wilbur had a pretty good operation," said the friend of the family. "That's some of the flattest land in the county. How could he let go of that?"

"Worked on his finances with him," said the banker. "You just can't make a living on 180 acres. Used to, but not anymore. You know he's been working at the lumber yard trying to pay off his debts. Told me it was killing him trying to do both, so he sold." He took a long drink of his cocktail. "And it could kill this county. Wilbur got a good chunk of change for that farm, which means the price of land will go up. We lose another family, because they're moving to Mahaska; and that means fewer kids, like Charles, in our schools, not as many people shopping on the square, not enough traffic to support our doctors and lawyers, although lawyers always seem to land on their feet." More laughter. "But I'm serious. It's going to hurt all of us here in town."

Charles was afraid they might ask him if he planned to live in Lockwood after college, so he quietly slipped from the group, only to be cornered by three somewhat tipsy men, including Mr. Blankenship who immediately lamented that Charles wasn't working this summer in the shoe store. "I already had to fire the kid who replaced you because he couldn't add, or get there on time." The three of them chuckled.

"It's the new math," said one of the others, a man Charles barely knew.

"Well, there's that," said Mr. Blankenship, "and then he just didn't look the part. Long hair, kind of scruffy. Charles is a good-looking young man. A little thin, but put a sport coat on him, with his short hair, he looks real professional." He downed his drink and pointed the glass at Charles. "What made you change your mind about staying in Lockwood? I thought you were going to work up at Drake this summer, and that's why you couldn't work in the store."

Charles mentally kicked himself for not having prepared a snappy response to this inevitable question. Before he could say anything, however, the other man said, "The bigger question is how you're getting along with Clyde. That man's meaner than a snake."

"No he's not!" said Charles sharply. "That's a prevalent misconception," a choice of words he regretted as soon as they left his mouth.

"'A prevalent misconception,'" the man echoed. "You sound like you've already started at that university." The three of them laughed.

"Maybe he seems mean," said the third man, "because he has to crack the whip to get any work out of those other two." He drained his glass and looked at the other adults. "You ever tried to talk to old Dexter and that one they call Moss? One's a windbag, and the other acts like he's deaf and dumb."

Charles could feel his stomach tighten and ears burn as he turned toward the large French doors that led to the parking lot. "You don't know what you're talking about! You don't know a thing about them! They care about this town. How many of you go to some other kid's Little League games? And they take pride in what they do, even though nobody notices. I bet they don't stand around talking about you, running you down. I bet they don't think about you at all."

That's what he wished he had said, the speech he rehearsed in his head as he walked, head down, past the high school, past the bank, past Blankenship's Shoes. It was not the first time he had walked home in recent days.

Chapter Four

Eaton's Grocery and General Store sits at the intersection of two county roads, about ten miles south of Lockwood as the crow flies. Clustered around it are a grain elevator, a Baptist church, and a half dozen houses that, taken together, are called Stiles. At one time, every hamlet in Savannah County had its own store; but by the time Charles was in high school, Eaton's was the only one left between Lockwood and the Missouri border.

Charles knew the store well because the Eatons were his great uncle, Claude, and his great aunt, Vera—who everyone, not just family, called "Auntie." It was Auntie who let him have baseball cards off the shelf when he was a kid, and even an occasional package of Twinkies. It was Auntie who fried catfish, his favorite, whenever the family came for a meal. It was Auntie who baked a cake—angel food, for Charles—for all of the family's birthdays. As he got older, however, what amazed Charles the most was that Auntie seemed genuinely nice to everyone who entered the store, including gruff old farmers and overly rambunctious children. When Reverend Shelton preached that people are basically good, it was Auntie who, in Charles' mind, came closest to confirming the theory.

His sister Connie's fourteenth birthday was actually on Friday, June 16, but Charles' parents decided to celebrate on Saturday (not Connie's preference) which, of course, included a trip to Stiles. Auntie and Claude's house, right next to the store, was undistinguished except for a porch that ran around two of its sides, and for the hydrangea bushes with blue, white, and pink globes of flowers that hugged the porch. As usual, Charles plopped down on the porch swing, which was comfortably covered by a frayed and faded quilt, and, as usual, Auntie soon joined him, full of questions. Was he excited about going off to college? Was he going to live in a dorm? Would he have a roommate? Was he still planning to major in history? ("Your father got his love of history from your grandfather, but I didn't get that part of the family inheritance. I just got a love of food," this said while patting her expansive waistline.) And how was his experience working on the street crew? After answering, Charles realized he had a question of his own: about the rural school that used to be in this part of the county, and whether she knew a man who used to teach there named Moss. But at that moment, Auntie was needed in the kitchen.

The festive dinner—chicken for the others, catfish that Claude caught for Charles—was served in what Auntie and Claude called their "shelter house," a screened-in, single-room

72

structure behind their home where they could eat without being eaten by mosquitoes. While the women prepared the meal of fried chicken and catfish, cole slaw, homemade rolls, cucumbers and tomatoes (the first of the summer), a corn casserole, and mashed potatoes with homemade egg noodles in chicken broth on top (a southern Iowa dish that Charles' mother could never get used to), the men churned the homemade ice cream, alternating salt and ice until it was too hard to crank. This year, however, when his father declared "Well, I believe that'll do it," Charles grabbed the handle from him, put his foot on the top, and turned it two more rotations.

After too much food was consumed, no one was in a hurry to clear the dishes, so they just sat, listening to the thrum of insects and watching the lightening bugs that flickered in the grassy area between the shelter house and the store. "I remember," said Auntie, "when you two were no bigger than a minute, catching bugs in a jar right here beside the garden."

"Those early tomatoes from your garden are sure good," said Claude's sister, and others agreed.

"Remember," said her husband, "when everybody around here had their own gardens? Hell, all the farms had their own eggs and milk and a pig or two to slaughter, so they didn't need to go runnin' to the store every ten minutes."

"Now Ed," said Auntie, "we *like* people coming often to the store," and they all chuckled. "Our problem is that people are leaving the farms."

73

"It's too damn hard to farm these days," said Ed. "People used to love it—hell, I used to love it—because you could be your own boss. Now some company like DeKalb tells us what to plant, we have to borrow money from old Clarence at the bank to buy equipment, equipment we need to keep up, and then end up relyin' on the government to pay us for leavin' ground fallow. What's free about that? Prices are the same this year as last, but expenses sure as hell keep going up. That's why I got out when I did. Came a point when workin' hard wasn't enough."

Again, there was agreement in the room as the women swung into action, stacking plates and setting out new ones for the birthday cake and ice cream. "I wish we had a piano out here," said Auntie, "so Charles could lead us," but they managed "Happy Birthday to You" a cappella. It was now dark enough that the crickets were in full chorus and they could see bugs swarming around the outside lights, some with hard shells occasionally hitting the screen surrounding them.

As soon as they were all settled with cake, and Connie had opened her presents, Charles' mother said how thankful they should be not to have a young man from their family in Vietnam. "Lots of families couldn't be celebrating tonight because they've got boys over there, or coming home dead."

When no one picked up on this conversation starter, Charles' father asked, "Claude, how long you think you'll be able to keep the store open?"

74

"As long as we can," Auntie answered. "Long as we have our health, which, knock on wood," she tapped on her chair, "is pretty good. At least that's what Dr. Amos told us last time we were in to see him."

Claude sat nodding before saying, "But it's probably good we're getting older. People would rather shop up on the square in Lockwood where they have more choices."

"Not even there," said Charles' father. "Now they'd rather go to Mahaska, even Des Moines. Blankenship tells me he's thinking about closing. The town may die before I do."

His aunt threw up her hands, but with a wide smile. "Oh, Robert! You always did think the sky's falling. Your grandfather was farming this county when the east side of the square burned, and people said that was the end of Lockwood. And then they hollered during the Depression that the town wouldn't survive, and then when we lost the train service. But things don't change that much. I bet it's doing fine long after we're all gone. Stiles won't be here, Eaton's Grocery won't be here, but Lockwood will."

Charles wanted to contribute to this conversation, but was having trouble getting his thoughts in order. He wanted to tell them that this summer he was working with people who cared about the town more than he ever imagined. At the same time, he had seen a split in the town he never before recognized. But what if he said these things and Ed began to make fun of the street crew the way the men had at the Country Club? As he was about to speak, formulating the words carefully in his head, he heard Auntie say, "At least we can be thankful we don't live in Detroit. Those people should be grateful for what they have instead of tearing it up."

"I hear the coloreds rip the plumbing out of some of those buildings," said Ed. "What good does that do anybody? Down here, at least we have enough goddamn sense to take care of what we got."

When it came to Charles' work with the street crew, the last two weeks of June were typical for their lack of routine. For a couple of days, all of them filled in holes around town with asphalt which, according to his father, "is worse than useless since the asphalt just wears away, leaving a hole bigger than before. I've said this to Clyde in council meetings, and he just keeps doing it." Then Charles and Jerry spent a day cutting weeds around the base of the water tower, which no one paid any attention to, except to complain when the weeds got too high. Then, while Jerry helped Moss with something, Charles helped Dexter replace part of the sidewalk in front of Harry's Hardware, his first time mixing concrete.

For the first three weeks or so, he spent the lunch hour walking home, eating the sandwich his mother had ready, and walking back. This, however, began to feel like a lot of wasted effort, so he and Jerry spent a week eating at the West Side Café, which quickly felt like a lot of wasted money. So both of them began bringing a lunch, which they ate in the garage with the others, sitting on the sagging couch or leaning against the dump truck, dust and pipe smoke hanging in the shafts of light cutting through the room. Charles noticed that Clyde often shared what he brought with Dexter, complaining all the while that his wife packed too much food in his metal lunch box. But when Charles offered half a sandwich, saying his mother had given him too much, Dexter said quietly, "Couldn't eat 'nother bite."

The days turned hotter, heat seeming to shimmer above the pavement, and he found himself thinking fondly of the air-conditioning in Blankenship's Shoes. Then, he and Jerry spent an even hotter day unloading lime at the water treatment plant. When Charles picked up the first fifty-pound bag, he wondered how he could possibly do this all day. To his surprise, however, it got easier, until his muscles gave out around 3:00, and Jerry had to unload the last of the truck by himself. For the next couple of days, Charles' arms and shoulders hurt so much he could hardly lift them; but this, he decided, was a sign his muscles were growing.

He had been coming to work in a uniform of T-shirt, jeans, baseball cap, and tennis shoes, but after dropping a bag of cement on his foot, he decided to buy a pair of work boots, which he was astonished to discover cost nearly a week's pay. Rather than buy them at Blankenship's on the square, he borrowed his mother's car and drove to Mahaska on a Saturday afternoon, and while there, since she had given him forty-five dollars, bought a pair of brown denim work pants with pockets big enough to hold small tools. He added a denim shirt to his pile of purchases, but then changed his mind. Maybe, he decided, his arms didn't need to be covered up after all. He was even getting a tan.

"I see," said Clyde the following Monday, "that one of you two's decided to be a worker."

"Shorts and tennis shoes suit me just fine," said Jerry.

"'To thine own self be true,'" said Moss.

Clyde stared at both of them, and then turned back to Charles. "'Course, you could just get yourself a pair of overalls, like Dexter here. You was born in overalls, wasn't you, Dexter?" Dexter stopped smoking long enough to grin. "Now Moss, he's tryin' to look like a real worker, with his official work pants and work shirts, all rolled up to the elbow. But people ain't fooled by the outfit." Dexter grinned, and Moss looked hurt or worried (Charles couldn't tell which) and started to protest, but Clyde cut him off. "I'm just joshin' ya, Moss. I remember that time you pert near broke a sweat." Dexter slapped his leg, spilling pipe tobacco all over the workbench in the process. Charles couldn't quite hear what Moss muttered under his breath, but the last words sounded like "scurvy companion."

These last two weeks of June were noteworthy in that Charles didn't go to church. He had been a regular at Lockwood Christian for as long as he could remember, so when he skipped two Sunday mornings in a row—frowned on by his father,

78

encouraged by his mother who said he needed the rest—he got a Sunday afternoon call from Reverend Shelton. Would he stop by the church some day that week, perhaps right after work? "Just to see how things are going for you this summer." Charles said something about getting back to him, but the next day Reverend Shelton happened to be on the corner in front of the West Side Café as Charles was headed home. The reverend suggested they get a Coke before the café closed, but Charles, who had perspired more than usual in his heavy work pants, said he smelled too bad to go where people ate, so they ended up on a bench under trees near the courthouse.

"This is actually one of my favorite places," said Reverend Shelton. "I like it better than the park, because there are a lot more people here on the square. When it really gets busy, like on a holiday weekend, when the farmers come to town and the Amish set up their tables with stuff from their gardens and those pies they bake—oh, boy!—it feels to me like an old-time market."

"A medieval market," said Charles. "I used to pretend that the courthouse was a medieval castle, with a moat all around it." He pointed to the streets that formed the square.

"As I recall, you used to say our church is like a medieval cathedral."

Charles smiled. "You're the one who pointed out our vaulted ceiling and round, stained-glass window. That's why I put a picture of our church in my research paper on cathedrals. And it did look like one when I was a kid. But now it feels pretty small."

"Strange how that works. On Sundays when we have low attendance, the sanctuary feels too big to me."

A breeze came up, and they sat for a minute enjoying it. "A castle is a good image," said the reverend at last, "for a kid. Castles keep us safe from what's outside." He shifted on the bench, turning more toward Charles. "But you're getting ready to go far beyond the moat. It seems to me that castle is now the wrong image."

Charles wasn't sure how to respond to that, so he said, "It's funny. Now that I'm ready to leave, I'm beginning to feel more here than I ever have."

They sat again in silence, until Reverend Shelton asked, "So, you like the people you're working with on the street crew?" Charles nodded.

"Maybe," said the minister, "that's actually a sign that you're stepping beyond the moat."

The last two weeks of June were also important for Charles because Clyde let him drive the tractor—in fact, invited him, encouraged him, to do so. After minimal instruction and a few awkward first attempts, Charles found himself scooping gravel into the back of the pickup and using the bucket to smooth the ground after they had filled in around a culvert. He even dug a short ditch using the backhoe. It felt natural, something physical he could do well. He took particular pride in backing the tractor into the garage, which had to be done at an angle in order to accommodate various items stacked up inside. That is until Friday, the last day of June, as they were shutting things down, when he cut it too sharply, catching the corner of the bucket on the track of the overhead sliding door and ripping a large section off the door frame.

Charles sat frozen in the seat of the tractor while the others gathered to survey the damage. "Clyde," he finally said, "I'm really sorry! I'll put it back up."

Clyde stared at the dangling track, slowly taking the pipe from his mouth. "You know how to fix somethin' like that, do ya? You know where we keep the lag screws, what to do if that cable there's off the roller, if the rail's bent? Huh? Your daddy teach you all that when he showed you how to rake?"

When Charles didn't respond, Dexter said he reckoned they could get it fixed pretty quick, but Clyde shook his head. "You go on home. Charlie's gonna learn a little carpentry." And so, after the others left, he and Clyde got to work, moving the tractor out of the way (Clyde insisting that Charles drive it), pulling two old ladders Charles had never seen from a corner of the garage, and lining up the screws and tools they would need. Then, with Charles mostly holding and Clyde mostly pounding and screwing, they began the laborious repair.

After an hour or so, Clyde stopped to let Charles tell his mother he wouldn't be home for dinner, and to refill his pipe.

81

Since there was no phone in the garage and the city office next door was closed, Charles wasn't sure where he could make a call; but not wanting to look like an even bigger dummy, he headed up the short hill to see what might be open on the square. To his surprise, Ginny was still in the West Side Café, putting chicken and potato salad on a plate, even though the café wasn't open for dinner. After he had used the phone, leaving a message with Connie, Ginny handed him two apples *to keep you going,* and let him out the locked front door. He didn't ask why she was fixing a dinner or who it was for or why the sheriff's patrol car was parked in front.

When Charles got back to the garage, he found Clyde sitting on one end of the couch, so bent over at the waist that his head nearly rested on his knees. "You okay?" he asked.

Clyde straightened quickly. "Just not as young as I used to be." Charles handed him an apple, while making yet another apology that Clyde dismissed with a flip of his hand. He carved the apple into slices with a pocket knife, and, after putting the first one in his mouth, asked, "Why're you goin' to Drake?"

"It's a good school," said Charles. "And it gets me out of Lockwood."

Clyde chewed another piece of the apple. "Seems to me it's awful close to home. Not much more'n a hundred miles from here to Des Moines, less if ya follow the river up through New Holland. You could go 'bout anywhere, from what I hear." This was not what Charles had expected, and so he said nothing before Clyde asked, "Where'd your dad go to college?"

"Yeah, he went to Drake," said Charles, defensively. And then, after a pause, "I think my minister wonders the same thing."

Clyde finished the apple and lit his pipe. Since the boss didn't seem in any hurry to get up, Charles decided to change the subject. "Moss told me you're not from Lockwood. Was it Wyoming?"

"Montana. He prob'ly was tellin' ya how I grew up around horses, and that's why I'm all bowlegged." Clyde took the pipe from his mouth and smiled, and Charles could actually feel himself, maybe both of them, relax. He settled back against the fender of the dump truck. "Dad had a ranch, small one. Not many horses, but enough it took a lot of work, 'cause we didn't have any help. He'd tell us boys to get up at 4:00, and if he had to come back, it was with the horsewhip."

"Why did you—?"

"Military."

"Did you fight in World War II? Moss said—"

"After that I started drivin' big equipment for Peter Kiewit. Government was buildin' roads everywhere. I'd level a roadbed, and then, if the sides needed it, I'd slide that grader down the slopes to get 'em smooth. That'll stir up the juices, I tell ya." He smiled, apparently at the memory, and took a puff. "Traveled all over doin' that. A big country."

Clyde looked as if he might stand up, so Charles asked quickly, "How did you end . . . what brought you to Lockwood?"

"Got roots here," said Clyde. "Dad moved away—run away, prob'ly—but Grandpa, he had a farm up near Martinsville, so I'd been here some. Wife come here with me when Grandpa died. Looked 'round and said she thought it'd be a good place to raise kids." His pipe had gone out, so Clyde knocked it on the side of the couch until the ash was all on the cement floor. "But now one of my boys, Scott, he seems like he's stuck here. And I don't know 'bout my girl, Frankie. Don't know what she's thinkin' these days. All I'm sayin' is it's good for kids to get away, see somethin' before they get where they're gonna end up."

He stood up and adjusted his hat. "We got to finish this. 'Nother hour'll do it." But he didn't move. "There used to be somethin' special 'bout this county. I said, 'Sure, I can quit movin' all over the country for Peter Kiewit and settle down here.' But now things here, they're all changin' and gettin' just like every other place. Hell, when I was in California, I seen corn big as we get here. Bigger. And before long we're gonna have the same problems they got there. The world's gettin' hard to figure."

It was nearly 10:00 when Charles got home. He could see the light in his parents' bedroom, but, instead of announcing his arrival, he went straight to the kitchen to fix a sandwich. It was there that his mother found him, eating at the kitchen table, and asked, "What happened? Was there some kind of emergency in town?" He briefly recounted the accident, emphasizing how Clyde had stayed to help him put the track back on the door frame—which was true, if you reversed it.

"Didn't Drake send you a list of books to read over the summer?" Charles could see where this was headed, so said nothing. "Well, maybe tomorrow you can do some of that reading. Or read something in French. *Étudies-tu votre français?*"

"*Je travaille demain matin.* I work *every* Saturday morning, on the street crew."

"Charles, you just got home! What's that make it, a seventeen-hour day?"

Charles slid his chair back and got up quickly. "I never get it right! First, Dad tells me to toughen up, work hard, be more what? . . . energetic, and then you tell me to sit around and read. Which is it? I'm doing what I agreed to do for the summer. Okay?" Then, in a softer voice, he added, "That reading list was just suggested, anyway, and I've already read some of them."

His mother said nothing until Charles, avoiding eye contact, had rinsed his dishes in the sink. "Yes, your grandmother pounded that into his head, so he's still out digging weeds or raking leaves when he could be doing something else."

"Maybe he likes digging weeds," said Charles. "Maybe I like helping Moss pick up trash around the square." He started to leave the kitchen.

"Connie said she saw you flexing your muscles, like some body builder, in front of the hall mirror." Charles could feel his ears burn, and his mother seemed immediately to regret this disclosure. "It's good . . . I'm glad you feel good about yourself . . . this way. All I'm saying is that you need to be flexing your brain, as well. Read a history book. Read *Moby Dick*. Read *Lady Chatterley's Lover*, for God's sake! That will be more useful when you're a professor or a lawyer someday than digging holes or whatever you do on the street crew."

He started again to leave the kitchen, but she wasn't finished. "Diane told me she heard people calling you Charlie."

"So you have a spy in the house *and* a spy downtown?" When his mother didn't respond, he added, "Yeah, that's what the whole crew calls me, except Jerry."

"But you hate the name Charlie! *I* hate the name Charlie! No one has ever called you that. When you were little, your grandmother started to, but I stopped it fast."

"Going by Charles wouldn't be right down there."

"But you are only down there, as you say, for three months, at the most."

"Then I will go back to being full-time Charles at Drake. What's the big deal?"

"This whole idea of working on the street crew was crazy from the beginning. You're not even seeing Nancy, so I don't know why you are even here this summer."

86

"Everyone," said Charles, "seems to think I should go away."

The Fourth of July was, of course, a holiday for city employees, but to the dismay of Charles' mother, the street crew worked on Monday the 3rd, though only until noon. Clyde started the day by setting off a string of firecrackers behind the couch while the boys were on it, sending them and dust flying, much to Dexter's amusement. Jerry told Charles that two can play this game and tossed a cherry bomb under the workbench, which nearly made Dexter lose his balance and all the tobacco in his pipe. Charles started to say that fireworks in a garage with paint thinner and gas-powered vehicles wasn't such a great idea—it could blow the place apart—but since Clyde clearly didn't mind, he held his peace.

Someone (not the street crew) put red, white, and blue bunting on the lampposts around the square every Independence Day; but this year there were also flags lining the walkway to the courthouse, and a large banner that read "Happy Birthday USA and Lockwood" above the main entrance, because the county had another reason to celebrate: it was the 125th anniversary of Lockwood's incorporation. In 1843, three years before statehood, the fifty inhabitants in this part of the Iowa territory declared themselves to be a town. Actually, 1967 was 124 years after that momentous event, but Mayor Kincaid was leaving office the next year and wanted the celebration to happen on his watch. This, he announced in the local paper, will be our quasquicentennial year, and Charles' father laughed out loud when he overheard someone wondering if this referred to an Indian tribe.

Charles asked Jerry if he was going to watch the anniversary/birthday parade on Saturday afternoon, but then tried to make the question seem like a joke when Jerry looked at him as if he were nuts. Perhaps for that reason, he arrived late to the parade, which actually didn't last more than a half hour. At his father's insistence, he was in time, however, for the mayor's speech. To his surprise, hundreds of people gathered around a makeshift platform on the courthouse lawn. For those who couldn't stand that long, folding chairs were set up in the shade of the few remaining trees. Commemorative programs were handed out all around, and were soon littering the grounds.

After the high school band played "The Star-Spangled Banner," the presentation began with applause for the veterans in the crowd and a moment of silence to remember soldiers killed or wounded in Vietnam, including one young man whose family lived in Martinsville. "People think towns like this are dying," said the mayor when it was his turn to speak. "Well, we are here and better than ever," which was met with scattered applause. "I know, it's easy and popular to talk and talk and talk about all the problems, and sometimes they do seem to come one right after another after another. But we also have a great history that sets the stage for an even greater future!" This led to a lengthy reflection on how the courthouse, built in 1877, would have gone up in flames during the fire of 1893 if it hadn't been made of sturdy material, just like the people of this county. "And if Rupert Haynes hadn't rushed into the hardware store, where Harry's is now, to get the dynamite caps they had in there, this whole square would have blown sky high." While Charles tried to remain attentive, all he could think about was who would have to clean up this mess once the crowd went home.

That evening, the Country Club had its annual Fourth of July fireworks extravaganza. As a kid, Charles had been part of the gallery on the clubhouse porch, oohing and aahing and clapping as sparkling colors burst over a pond alongside the second fairway. For the past two years, he had helped set them off. This year, however, he skipped the event altogether, telling his mother he was going to stay home and read *Lady Chatterley's Lover*.

Perhaps this history is what made Charles so incensed when next morning he discovered that, while volunteers were cleaning up the mess on the square, the street crew was expected to clean up the debris around the pond. "Why can't the Country Club clean up its own mess?!" he demanded to know. "They shot it off, they ought to pick it up." Moss told him he should be grateful for an easy day, because tomorrow they would be back to oiling streets. Clyde seemed slightly amused at his indignation. "The Club," he said when Charles had finished ranting, "says they put on their fireworks shindig for the entertainment of the town, so the town should say thankee by cleanin' it up." Charles started to ask if Clyde or Dexter or Moss had ever been in the clubhouse, let alone played a round of golf, but thought better of it and confined his grumbling for the rest of the day to Jerry.

Sure enough, when Charles got to the garage on Thursday, the spacesuits were spread out on the workbench. Dexter backed the dump truck, already filled with sand, out the good-as-new sliding door so that Clyde could get the sand spreader from the top of the storage shelves, using a forklift borrowed from somewhere. "Why do you keep it way up there?" Jerry asked him.

"You see any room for it down here? There ain't any 'cause this garage is too damn small. Only place for it on the shelves is up near the ceiling. Lower ones are too narrow. So when we need it, we just get this forklift and lift 'er down."

Once it was off the shelves and Clyde gave the word, he, Dexter, Moss, and Jerry carried the heavy, unwieldy sand spreader to the back of the truck, and, on his count, hoisted it to the top of the tailgate where Charles was ready to let them know when it was in place. But as Charles looked on, unable to help, the spreader began to tilt in Clyde's direction. He heard Dexter yell "Watch 'er!" and Jerry shout something about not being able to hold it, as the spreader lurched sideways, knocking Clyde to the pavement and landing, with a loud clatter, on cement and the side of his left leg.

The three of them lifted the spreader quickly, as Charles clambered off the truck. They all wanted to call the town's ambulance, but Clyde, who was in obvious pain, wouldn't hear of it. He did, however, let them help him into the city's pickup and allow Dexter to drive him to the hospital, where the four of them waited until Clyde's wife appeared and told them that Clyde said they should go do some work for a change.

"Clyde's strong as a mule," said Jerry, once they were back in the garage. "I guess he just lost his grip, and then I couldn't hold it up. That thing must weigh over three hundred pounds."

"More'n that," said Dexter.

"Maybe he was just tired," said Moss. "He's been worried about his children, like Lear about his daughters."

"Or," said Dexter, "he ain't quite right," which is when Charles told them how he had found Clyde slumped over the night the two of them had stayed late to fix the door. Dexter shook his head while Charles was talking and looked sad. "Better not to tell 'bout some things," he said, "outside this here garage."

Chapter Five

Even Charles knew that one of the reasons Iowa grows so much corn and soybeans is the often complained-about weather. For as long as he could remember, his mother had grumbled that the humidity frizzed her hair and put the piano out of tune. And now he found that the inside rim of his baseball cap was soaked before he had worked an hour. There wasn't a day that Moss didn't compare their heavy air to that of the jungles he had taught about at his school in the country, and even Clyde admitted that it wore on him. "It'd be sticky here anyways," he said one day as they were filling in holes, "but sweat off the corn makes it worse." Charles wasn't sure he bought that theory, one he'd also heard from his grandfather, but there was no doubt the Iowa weather had wilted his California cousins the year they came to visit in July. The cousins had also been shocked to discover that in Iowa it rains in the summer, usually in the form of thunderstorms that typically come at night.

Twice, that Charles could recall, tornadoes had touched down in Savannah County. One of them took a strip out of a cornfield like a lawn mower takes out of a yard. That, at least, was his father's analogy. The other destroyed a barn northeast of Lockwood, and ripped the roof off the farmhouse while the family huddled in the backyard root cellar. Charles' father had taken him along to survey the damage, which led his mother to accuse her husband of being no better than those lawyers who chase ambulances.

Despite all of this, Charles actually liked thunderstorms. He liked the feeling in the air before a storm, how you could smell the change coming. And now that he was working, he especially liked the mornings after it rained. Since it wasn't possible to do many of their usual tasks, the crew would sit a little longer in the garage. And when Clyde did rouse them to action, he would tell the college boys to ride around town in the pickup, clearing out the debris that had washed into the storm drains. Generally, this was leaves and small branches, but they also found such things as plastic sandbox toys, a Wiffle ball, sunglasses, and a pair of women's underwear, which led Jerry to speculate on the possible explanations, until Charles was sick of hearing someone else's fantasies.

Sometimes, however, a storm would blow up in the afternoon, clouds gathering ominously in the west, lightening flashing in the distance, like an army preparing to attack. When this happened at the beginning of the second week in July, the garbage crew also headed for cover. That's why eight of them were congregated around the couch and workbench as the storm hit, sending sheets of rain against the west-facing door, one crack

94

of thunder sounding very near their refuge. The storm darkened the garage, so Clyde pulled the chain that turned on the single light bulb hanging above the bench.

"This one'll pass," said Chuck from the garbage crew, "but we're due for a big one. Haven't had a tree buster in three years."

Charles and Jerry often sat on the couch next to Clyde, but now Clyde had his heavily-bandaged left leg stretched across the middle of the cushions, and they instinctively left the other end for Henry, a member of the garbage crew who was not much over fifty, but seemed older. "Clyde, this rain's a gift," said Chuck, who always sounded as if he were shouting over the roar of a truck. "You need time to rest."

"The leg's nothin'," said Clyde. "They'll take these band-aids off before ya know it."

"I'm not talking about your leg. From what I hear, this boy's been making you work to midnight just to fix things he hits with that tractor." The other two garbage crew guys, Marvin and Henry, chuckled, but Charles noticed that Clyde barely smiled and Dexter didn't slap his knee.

"And I reckon," said Clyde, "you ain't made no mistakes in your glorious career."

Chuck leaned his considerable bulk against the workbench and gestured toward Charles and Jerry. "Well, these boys, they'll go back to college and forget what real work's like, anyway."

"As if you'd know what real work's like," said Marvin, "sittin' up there on your padded seat while Henry and me lift the cans. The only muscle you use is the one in your ass." This time they all laughed, including Chuck, and Dexter slapped his knee.

"I put in my time," said Chuck. "I lifted those cans before we got this fancy new truck, back when you had to empty 'em over the side. Moss, he even did it with me for most of a year." He paused, in a way that indicated he had more to say, and no one interrupted. "I'm not just talking about working on the streets. I'm talking about farming and construction, like bricklaying. The whole country's becoming too goddamn soft. Honest work like we do, nobody gives a shit about anymore. They go to school, and keep going to school, so's they won't have to get drafted or get a real job."

"The value of education—" Moss started, but Clyde cut him off.

"All I know is I wished I'd went to college." There was silence as he knocked ash from his pipe. "Muscles only gets you so far."

"It got your boys pretty far," said Marvin. "How many wrestling trophies they got between 'em?"

Clyde waved his pipe dismissively. "Yeah, and now what? Wrasslin' don't buy eggs and bacon." He knocked his pipe again on the side of the couch. "One of those wrasslers is now back livin' under my roof 'cause his head ain't screwed on straight. Got a daughter who's smart enough, but she's still there, too."

He pointed at Charles. "This boy's got some things to learn 'bout tractors, but his head's screwed on straight."

"I understand if there's some resentment about college kids," said Jerry, "since we get a deferment from the military." Charles usually admired Jerry's confident candor, but this comment struck him as unhelpfully honest. And this feeling was confirmed when Henry, silent until now, began to speak, at first so low that Charles, standing by the dump truck, had to strain to hear him.

"I'll tell you what I know about it. I know there's no bandages that'll fix my boy's leg. Not worth a damn. Never will be worth a damn. Sits in the pool hall all day, leg stretched out like Clyde's." His voice grew louder. "All I know about it is if I could get my hands on that college-educated" (he spit the words like an expletive) "lieutenant who ordered him to go up that goddamn trail where he knew goddamn well the Vietcong was waiting—Hank says every one of 'em knew it for certain—if I could get my hands on him . . . I'd tear him apart 'til there's no scraps to put on our truck!" Henry's face was red as he slumped on the couch. "That's all I know about it," his voice again barely audible.

It was Clyde who broke the silence that followed. "It ain't the college."

"What?" said Henry.

Clyde looked at him across the couch. "I said it ain't the college. There's fools in this world, and ones that ain't fools. College can't help a fool, but it sure as hell can help the others."

That evening, Charles was in a sour mood, made worse by his sister. He was in the kitchen, describing the day to his mother, including Clyde's leg stretched out on the couch, when Connie interrupted. "Remember when Mom had to rescue you from church camp because you scraped your knee or something, and then you sat around with it stretched out on the couch like you were really hurt?" Her smile reminded him of the Cheshire Cat.

"For your information, I didn't *scrape my knee*, I sprained my ankle! A bad sprain, and even Mom said they shouldn't have had us running an obstacle course in the first place."

When his mother stayed silent, Connie's smile grew even wider. "That's not what Dad had to say about it. He said you just wanted an excuse not to rough it, because you're not tough, even if you are still on the street crew."

"Why does she have to be such a pain?" Charles asked his mother, once Connie had fled his threatened attack.

"Because she's fourteen years old. And besides, imagine what it's like having every teacher expect you to be as smart as your brother. You're eighteen. Don't let her get to you. It just makes you sound like you're closer to fourteen than to twenty."

Charles thought of going to the basement, but since Connie was probably there, he wandered to his room, but the house felt claustrophobic. Jerry was with Sandy, and while Charles didn't feel like riding around with Randall and company, he also wasn't in the mood to stay home, partly because he kept picturing Jerry and Sandy in the backseat of the Camaro, and partly because the afternoon's work conversation, especially his reluctance to jump into it, kept replaying in his head. So he decided to go see Dexter.

Sure enough, Dexter was sitting in the lawn chair with its loose-hanging strap, wearing his overalls over a once-white T-shirt with stains around the sagging neck, pipe in his mouth, transistor radio by his side on the stoop. Water dripped off the dented, metal awning as they listened to the Cardinals take an early lead, only to give it up in the seventh. Dexter shook his head as Harry Caray described the fiasco.

"You think they'll win the pennant?" asked Charles.

Dexter nodded a few times before saying, "Some nights I ain't sure." He took a puff on his pipe. "But, yep, believe they will. Gotta believe they will."

To make conversation, Charles talked about some of the games he had seen in St. Louis with his family and, more recently, his friends. He then told about going with his parents to watch the Cubs play in Chicago, before remembering that Dexter had never seen a Major League game. He stopped himself just as he was about to describe the Hilton on Michigan Avenue where they stayed.

Dexter, however, just smoked and occasionally nodded, rocking slightly as if his lawn chair were a front porch swing. Then, to Charles' surprise, he asked, "You readin' books?"

"Well, I'm not reading as much this summer as my Mom thinks I should. She was a teacher, at least for a while, and she wants me to be a professor, or something like that."

Dexter nodded, puffing occasionally on his pipe. "I read some."

Why, Charles wondered, did this so amaze him? He tried not to show it as he asked, "What do you like to read, Dexter?"

Two puffs on the pipe. "Clyde, he give me some magazines. *National Geography.*"

"I think you mean—"

"He give me one 'bout the Ozarks."

They sat quietly listening to the Cardinals, and again it was Dexter who broke their silence. "What d'ya do when you go home of an evening?"

"Jerry and I go out some. Ride around. And I help my dad. He's always got some job or other for me to do. *No sitting around!* That's his motto." Dexter nodded. "I do read some," Charles added. "Practice the piano, if I'm bored enough."

Dexter took the pipe from his mouth and smiled his brown, jagged smile. "I got a piano."

"Really?! Why . . ." He stopped. "I mean, is it here in your house?"

Dexter got slowly to his feet, and, after Charles had followed him to the backyard, pulled up a corner of the rain-slicked tarp to reveal an old upright. Even in the fading light, Charles could make out large scrapes across the top and a chunk missing near the bottom. "The hotel put it in the alley, so Moss and me, we put 'er in the truck." He smiled again. "We asked 'em 'bout the seat, but guess they lost it." Charles reached out to the keyboard, but the first key he hit simply thunked. "It's broke," said Dexter, "but Moss, he thinks somebody can fix it." Pause. "Maybe you."

"I don't know how to fix a piano!" Then, seeing Dexter look down at his feet, Charles said, "But, yes, there are people who do that kind of thing."

"It's goin' in the place in the Ozarks." Pause. "Makes a place special."

"But, Dexter, you can't keep it here. It's going to get completely . . . it's going to get so nobody can fix it."

Charles could now barely see Dexter who was staring at the stem of his pipe. "Can't get it in the house."

"I know what we can do!" Charles exclaimed. "We can put it in a corner of the garage at my house, my dad's house." Even in the fading twilight, Charles could see that Dexter looked uncomfortable. "No, really, it wouldn't be in the way."

The next evening, however, when he gently raised the topic, his mother said, "Of course not," and his father simply said, "No." Charles persisted. He had *promised* Dexter. It wouldn't make any difference to them, they wouldn't know it was there, and it would make a big difference to Dexter. Finally, after conferring in the kitchen, his parents agreed he could put it in the utility shed with the riding mower and other tools.

A day later, Dexter said nothing as Charles and Jerry struggled to get the piano into the bed of the city pickup, a task made harder than it should have been by the broken tailgate. With Charles in the back, holding tightly to the piano, Jerry slowly drove the nine blocks to the big house on Chestnut. In the early evening sunlight, Charles could see that the piano was in worse shape than he had imagined, with initials and two hearts carved on one side. They covered it with an old quilt his mother no longer used and slid it into a back corner of the shed.

That night the big one hit. Charles got little sleep once the thunder began to rumble and crack and the wind lashed rain against the house. Just when he thought the worst had passed, the wind would pick up and the rain become torrential. He imagined branches of the dying elm breaking off and crashing into the utility shed and Dexter's piano. Twice he got up to peer out his window overlooking the backyard, but even when the lightening flashed he couldn't see the shed because of the rain and the branches of a tree near the house that thrashed about wildly in the storm.

When morning came, the tree and shed were intact, but Charles was still startled at the extent of the damage, which, it occurred to him, he now saw through different eyes. Chestnut Street was littered with small branches, as were the yards of the large homes near his parents. An ornamental stand had toppled in front of one of them, smashing ceramic pots across the porch.

As he neared the square on foot, he could see there was far more damage in the direction of his church. He walked toward it and discovered that lightening had apparently hit a large maple, splitting off several sizeable limbs that not only blocked the street, but crumpled the hood of a car on the other side. Debris was piled against the fence surrounding the grade school, and a sign in front of the school was dangling precariously.

Having seen enough, Charles hurried to the garage, anxious to find out about Dexter, who, it turned out, wasn't there. "Seems his tarp flapped around pretty good," said Clyde, "so I told him he should clean up 'round there before he comes in."

"So you already saw him this morning?"

"Went by last night," said Clyde, filling his pipe. "His house ain't very tight, so I tried to get him and his missus to come over to our place, but he said she was too sickly to come out."

"You checked on him in the middle—"

Clyde cut him off. "'Round here, if it ain't one thing, it's another. I remember one time we had hail so hard thought I was back in the war. That metal thing over Dexter's door, that's when it got all beat up. Seemed to get the worst of it."

This time it appeared an area by the fairgrounds got the worst of it, so Clyde announced that he and Moss would head there with the tractor to move trees blocking a couple of streets. "Even with my leg all wrapped up, I can drive the tractor. And that'll help the pole climbers get the power back on out that way."

"What happens," said Jerry with a big smile, "when someone from the Country Club calls and wants us to move a tree that's across a fairway?"

"I'll tell 'em to go fuck 'emselves with one of the branches," said Clyde. They all laughed, and Charles was sorry Dexter wasn't there to slap his knee. "You two," he said to Charles and Jerry, "take the pickup and see what big stuff—branches, things like that—you can clear outta the streets. Start up by the hospital." He looked directly at Jerry. "But you don't have to do nothin' in the cemetery. Nobody's gettin' there in a hurry." Both of them smiled. "Don't do nothin' in people's yards neither, just streets and sidewalks. That's it. We'll have a brush pile out south of the fairgrounds, so when the pickup's full, take 'er there."

Clyde hobbled to a corner of the garage and pulled two small chainsaws off one of the shelves. This time he looked directly at Charles. "You know how to use one a these?" Charles nodded, but without much conviction, so Clyde said, "I want you cuttin' wood, not cuttin' you. Left hand up here in front by the brake, right hand by the throttle. Don't push down hard, just steady." He handed them both a pair of goggles, one more scratched than the other. "These'll make Jerry here feel right at home, like he's swimmin'." They all smiled.

At first, the job seemed overwhelming. After spending nearly an hour on one block near the hospital, they began to concentrate on branches big enough to require a chainsaw, ignoring everything else. Before long, Charles was getting the

104

hang of it. He found himself wishing that Randall, Cliff, and Kenny—or Nancy, for that matter—would drive by and see him in action: goggles in place, right hand on the throttle, left hand by the brake.

By lunchtime, they had already made three runs to the brush pile, the only problem coming when the truck was partially blocking the driveway of a woman who yelled that she needed to get out *now*. Charles thought she was so rude that they should only move it to the edge of the driveway; but Jerry of the perpetual smile hopped in the truck and moved it down the street, waving to the woman as he did so.

Mid-afternoon they were taking a break, leaning against the pickup, passing the city thermos back and forth, when a woman Charles knew from church approached them. "Oh, Charles," she said, "I thought that was you." Charles introduced Mrs. Cunningham to Jerry. "I was a friend of Charles' grandmother," she said, as if by way of explanation. "We grew up together in Lockwood, lived here all of our lives, were in the same bridge club, went to the same church, although I thought for a while she was going to be a Methodist . . . can you imagine? But now I'm ninety-two years old and all of my friends are gone. Dead. Can you believe it, ninety-two?! Almost ninety-three! Just two and a half weeks, July 29. Maybe they'll have a party at the church, if I can get there. There ought to be something—don't you think?—for people who live longer than their friends." Charles assured her they would have a party (although he couldn't recall any birthday parties there for old people); and he would be happy to pick her up and take her to the church.

"Oh," she said, "I still drive around town. Not on the highway, but to the store and to the church. Just not very fast. But now," pointing toward the driveway that ran along the side of her small, brick house, "I can't get out at all on account of that tree." Sure enough, a sizable branch lay across the driveway and part of her front yard, though not the sidewalk. "My nephew used to do things like that for me—you know him, Rudy—but now he has moved to Mahaska. He got a good job there in the John Deere factory, or so he says, but that doesn't help me much. So it would be a blessing if you young men could get rid of it for me. It will be forever before I can find someone I can pay to do it."

Charles took a deep breath and started to repeat Clyde's instructions, but before he got two words out, Jerry said, "Sure, we can do that." Turning to Charles, he added softly, "Clyde would, too, if he were here," and Charles decided this was probably true. They tried lifting the branch, simply to get it out of the way, but it was too heavy, so they cut it up and tossed the pieces in the bed of the truck.

When they were finished, sweat dripping from under Charles' cap, Mrs. Cunningham stood at the door of her house with two glasses of lemonade, which they gratefully accepted, and an 8 1/2 x 11 manila envelope, which Charles refused to accept. "We get paid by the city," he told her, "so we can't take

106

money from ordinary people," wishing immediately he could rephrase that sentence.

"Oh, it's not money, Charles. It's . . . well, it's just something to remember this day. You can open it later."

They picked up a few more branches on her street, while Mrs. Cunningham watched at a distance. Once they were on the next block, Jerry pulled the truck to the curb and Charles opened the envelope, which contained a large color photograph of Mrs. Cunningham. For the next half hour, they mused over this gift, wondering why an old lady would give a picture of herself to two young men who barely knew her.

But then, with the clock approaching 4:30, Charles slipped on the wet pavement while carrying a load of wood, and the sharp end of a hefty branch jabbed into his forearm. By the time Jerry came around the truck to see what had happened, blood had trickled down Charles' wrist and continued to bleed while they debated what to do. The hospital seemed like overkill; the wound wasn't that bad. Jerry could drive him home, but Charles doubted they had any gauze, and it needed more than a small bandage. Besides, Connie might tell people he came home early because he had a scrape. They could go to the garage, but God only knew what first-aid supplies were there, or what Clyde would have to say about it. Finally, they decided that Jerry would drop him off at Rexall Drugs on the north side of the square where he could get some gauze and mercurochrome.

Then he could just walk home from there, while Jerry took the last load to the brush pile and gave Clyde some explanation.

In the drugstore, Betsy the clerk insisted on washing the wound and bandaging it herself. "It's what your mother would do for Jeff," although Charles wasn't sure about that. Once she finished, Charles realized, with a flush of embarrassment, that he had no money. "Your dad's office is right upstairs," said Betsy, "and I know he's good for it."

The shortest way home was to turn right out of the drugstore, and then right at the corner on Chestnut; but Charles decided to go left out of the store in order, he told himself, to get a better look at storm damage off the northeast corner of the square. And he was in no hurry to see his sister or to have his mother lecture him about the dangers of working on the street crew.

The first shop he came to, walking east, was Blankenship's Shoes, which he hurried past, eyes on the sidewalk. When he raised them, he was in front of Fashion on the Square, and there in the window, arranging a blouse on a mannequin, was Clyde's daughter Frankie, her own blouse stretched tight as she reached around the inert model. Since there didn't seem to be anyone else in the store, and since he thought he heard someone opening the door of Blankenship's (Charles certainly didn't want to talk to him), he decided to go inside.

Frankie stepped from the window, smiling. "I've been waiting for *someone* to come in for the past hour, and who do I get but a guy from the street crew." When Charles didn't have a ready response, she asked, "So, what brings you in? Buying a dress for a girlfriend? Something summery that slips on and off real easy?"

She smiled, and Charles felt himself blushing. "No, I just saw you in the window and thought I'd say hi." That sounded lame, so he added, "Your dad talks about you a lot."

"*Does* he?" said Frankie, emphasizing the first word. "Well, I'm sure he talks to you more than he talks to me." Charles had been standing near a rack of dresses just inside the door. As she was speaking, Frankie took hold of his wrist and gently, but purposefully, guided him to an open area by the counter and cash register. He still could feel the coolness of her fingers after she let go. "It doesn't help business," she explained, "if the dresses smell like guys who hang out in gutters . . . or if you bleed all over them."

He saw she was now staring at his bandage, which had grown a big red spot in the middle. "What happened to you?" she asked. And so he told her, in detail he later decided was embarrassing, about the chainsaw and the brush pile and picking up limbs around town, until the very last one gashed him. "But at least today," he concluded, "we weren't hanging out in the gutter." Frankie smiled.

A woman Charles recognized as a friend of his mother's opened the door and walked in, but, after glancing around, walked right back out. Frankie had seemed ready to speak to her, but apparently decided against it. "By the way," she said, once

109

the woman was gone, "I'm used to the way you smell," a comment that caught Charles off guard, until he realized she was referring to Clyde. "So what does my father say about me to the guys on the street crew?"

How to respond? Finally he said, "You seem to be a mystery to him." Frankie laughed, but a fun laugh, not sarcastic. "But my parents," he added, "seem to think I'm a mystery to them, too."

"Really? You always struck me as a guy who gets along with his parents. Not somebody who has big secrets like some of . . . like some people." Again Charles wasn't sure what to say, and again Frankie laughed, gently. "Your parents seem nice, although your mom's hard to read and your dad does sometimes look like he could explode."

How did she . . .? "I'm not spying on your family," she added, as if reading his mind. "Your father works right down the block, you know." Again that smile, a very attractive smile, and that laugh, a very pleasant laugh.

And before he could consider the words fully, Charles found himself asking, "Would you like to do something, you know, with me, on Saturday? Get something to eat . . . or something? I promise to take a shower."

Instead of laughing, Frankie looked at him intently. There was an awkward pause before she said, "You know, Charles," this was the first time she had said his name, "it's interesting that you worked next door in Blankenship's all last summer, and I can't remember that we ever said hello. Your dad says hello to

110

me, but you didn't." She picked up a stack of folded blouses on the counter as she added, "I'm afraid I have plans for Saturday."

"Of course," said Charles. "What is this, Thursday? I should have . . . anyway, it was good to talk to you . . . Frankie."

He turned toward the door, careful to keep a respectful distance from the racks of dresses. As he took hold of the handle, he heard her move around the counter, and then heard her say, "But I think I can change them."

Chapter Six

As a middle-schooler, Charles had to learn about Iowa's ninety-nine counties, and, being the student he was, he learned them all in alphabetical order. Number 1: Adair. Number 2: Adams. Number 81: Savannah. Since the county number appeared vertically on the left-hand side of a license plate, Charles the child had the annoying (to his parents) habit of shouting out the origin of cars as they approached on the highway.

Charles could make his quick run to the Missouri border because Savannah is on the row of southernmost Iowa counties; and the tickly hills are a reminder of why it is one of the poorest. Hilly, tree-covered country is beautiful, even mysterious, but not great for farming. This is especially so where the Des Moines River cuts across the northeast corner of the county, and near Lake Winyan in the northwest.

A map produced by the Iowa Historical Society marks several places of interest in Savannah County, including the remnants of a Sauk Indian village; four farms that were robbed by Confederate raiders in October of 1864; the home of James B.

Highsmith, presidential candidate of the Greenback Party in 1880; and Mars Hill, the oldest log church in the state. The map for 1967 did not show the three farms newly-purchased by the Amish. "Mark my words," said Charles' father to anyone who would listen, "where there are three there will be more. I don't care which church people go to, but since they don't buy cars or insurance or clothes or paint, this does not bode well for the future of Savannah."

An aerial view of the county would show Lockwood smack in the center, with hamlets with names like Mason and West Valley and Stiles tucked in here and there. The one Charles heard mentioned most in July of 1967 was Martinsville, where a motorcycle gang set up camp in the park. Rumor had it that a couple of local boys were beaten up and one of the local girls molested. Some said they heard this directly from Woody, who claimed to have personally ushered the gang out of the county, although others said they hadn't heard anything about molesting, and thought the gang left on their own.

Charles stopped by the dress shop on Friday, again checking to make sure there were no customers, to confirm he would pick Frankie up on Saturday at 7:00, an hour he considered stylishly late. And if the evening was a bust, there would be less of it. Then, the image of Clyde lurking in the back of his mind, came the awkward question: *Where* should he pick her up? But before he could ask, Frankie said, "Why don't I meet you on the west side of the square."

Charles had asked his mother if he could borrow her Ford Fairlane, because it was sportier than his father's Buick, and she generally asked fewer questions about why he needed a car. On Saturday, he guided the Fairlane into a parking spot opposite the closed West Side Café shortly before 7:00, but Frankie was already there, partially hidden in the shadow of a tree near the courthouse. He hadn't told her what to expect, beyond that they were going to dinner, so she was dressed like someone on her way to church, in a conservative blouse and skirt that came nearly to her knees (did she get those, he wondered, at Fashion on the Square?), with a purse big enough to hold a book or two over her shoulder. "I thought," he told her as she slid into the passenger-side bucket seat, "that we could drive over to a place I know on the river by Red Rock."

She smiled slightly. "Over in Ponca County."

"Yeah, you know, get out of Lockwood. Some place different."

"Different than what? We've never—" She stopped. "Sure, Charles. Whatever you have planned."

As they drove out of town, Frankie asked how his arm was healing, but there is only so much to be said about a bandage. "I once . . ." she started, but then dropped it, instead asking if there was a lot of damage from the storm at his—his parents'—house. After that, she fell silent, perhaps because Charles was busy fiddling with the radio. He resisted tuning in the Cardinals in favor of a Top Ten station, whose playlist seemed creepily thematic: "Somebody to Love," "All You Need is Love." At one point, he turned the radio off, but then, when he wasn't sure what to talk about, turned it back on. Had it been this awkward with Nancy? He tried to remember their first date, but, in fact, he couldn't recall any of their conversations. "Sunshine of Your Love," "Baby, I Need Your Lovin'."

As they approached the river (a longer drive than Charles remembered), Frankie asked, "Do you like this music?"

"Yeah, I guess. What do you listen to?"

"Country, but this is fine. I doubt the buttons on this car are set for country." She looked at him and smiled.

The restaurant, it turned out, was full, and Charles, being a novice at adulthood, hadn't made a reservation. But as he was trying to decide what to do, a table opened up in a corner by the large window overlooking the river, and even though Charles thought he had seen that they were fourth on the list, the hostess led them to it.

"How's this?" he asked, not knowing quite what to say.

"It beats the Dairy Queen," said Frankie. They both smiled, and he saw in the glow of the sunset over the river that, not only did he like her smile, she was actually quite pretty. Tanned complexion, like Clyde's, even though she spent her days indoors. A bit stocky, like Clyde, but not too overweight. Brown,

116

shoulder-length hair that looked much fuller and wavier than he remembered from seeing her in the store.

A waitress brought menus, but instead of studying his, Charles began to ask questions he now felt he should have been asking in the car. I'm not picky about what I eat, she told him in response to one, immediately asking about his favorite foods. Yes, she liked going to Des Moines, although she hadn't been there often, immediately asking why he decided to go to Drake. Yes, she did like to read, although she didn't have as much time for it as she would like, immediately asking what were his favorite books. No, she didn't know any French, but she had taken a year of Spanish, immediately wanting to know what he found most interesting about the language.

"How do you like working at Fashion on the Square?"

"It's better than most of the options in Lockwood." She took a sip of water. "What's it like working with Jerry Hinkle?"

So he told her about tarring the streets and about painting the curbs on the square, including rolling along on the dollies. "I saw you," she said. "Remember? I came by during my break and said I liked your unusual technique." Oh yeah, he remembered, he assured her, quickly beginning to tell about cleaning up after the storm, noticing now how she kept her eyes focused on his. And her eyes were very attractive. *Very* attractive. Dark brown, probably like Clyde's.

Before he knew it, he found himself telling Frankie about the near-accident in the drainage ditch, something he had not told his parents or even Dexter. He was amazed at the detail of his own recounting: what he saw in the moonlight, the music on the tape deck, the sound of loose gravel, the rapidly approaching culvert, while Frankie listened quietly but intently, eyes on his. "I guess we were pretty lucky," he concluded.

"Or blessed." Not a word he expected.

"I keep thinking about people who screw up just one time and their life is ruined."

"It's not just a one-time thing." His look showed he didn't understand, so she added, "Some people, to use your word, are lucky where they're born or when they're born or who they're born to. That's a bigger thing than luck. They're blessed."

The waitress had brought them a stuffed celery appetizer, "compliments of the chef," and now she brought their salads. Frankie laughed, that same laugh he had heard in the store, and told him she wasn't used to food coming in stages. Charles started to say "courses," but stopped himself in time and asked, "What's it like growing up with two brothers who are—"

"Tough guys?" Again that smile. "People think Clyde only wanted boys, so he even named me like one. But that's not the way it is. I know he wanted a girl. I think he got tired of all the wrestling and . . . cussing." She took a bite, and then said, as if an afterthought, "I think he wanted them to be tough, at first, and when he wanted them to be something else, it was too late."

For Charles, the rest of the evening felt nearly magical. As the sun merged with the horizon, the hostess appeared with a candle, which sent flickering highlights across Frankie's face and hair. She ordered catfish, which she clearly savored. When he asked how it tasted, she handed him her fork and insisted he eat the bite that was on it. So he shared a bite of his chicken, and soon they were practically eating off each other's plates, as if she knew he would have ordered the catfish if she hadn't ordered it first. Even though he was worried about his cash on hand, Charles suggested they get dessert, which Frankie agreed to only if they could split something, and then picked the rhubarb pie, which happened to be the cheapest item on the menu.

They laughed out loud as she told stories of shoppers who claimed they wore a size ten when it would have been hard to squeeze them into a dress twice that size. "Deary," she said in the voice of an old woman, "are they changing the sizes on dresses these days?" One woman actually accused her of switching labels!

They laughed as Charles told how Clyde gave Jerry a hard time for wearing shorts to work. "This sand goes on the streets," said Charles, trying not very successfully to imitate Clyde. "Don't be confusin' it with some beach you go layin' on."

For a second, he was worried that Frankie would take offense at this mockery of her father, but she laughed loudly. "He hates short pants on men. Period," she told him. "Scott wore a pair once, and Clyde told people for a month he now had two daughters."

Then they laughed about high school teachers. Even though she had graduated two years before him, they had both had Mr. Bartholomew for history. It was Charles who recalled the day Mr. B showed up wearing two ties, one he had tied and one he apparently had forgotten was also around his neck. "I don't know where he came from," said Frankie, "but if they hired him, they must not have had any alternatives."

Frankie shook her head as Charles told about the two people, both of them north of the square, who wondered why the street crew hadn't yet picked up smaller branches on their property when a whole tree was uprooted near the fairgrounds and large limbs were down in other parts of Lockwood. But when Charles laughed about Mrs. Cunningham and her picture, Frankie said, "That's kind of funny, but it's also sweet. Everyone wants to be remembered, one way or another."

They sat staring out the window for a minute before Charles asked, "Did Clyde tell you how I ripped the track off the door frame trying to back the tractor in that garage?"

Frankie reached for her purse and rummaged in it while saying, "I heard him tell Mom something about an accident. But I didn't hear him say it was you . . . directly." Before Charles could ask what that meant, she added, "I had an accident with a tractor when I was a kid. Clyde said it should've killed me. So I guess I'm blessed, too, in a way."

"What happened? Were you hurt?"

"Oh, I'll save that for another time." She smiled and looked down. "You know . . . if you stop in the store again." Then, to his surprise, she reached across the table and lightly touched his birthmark.

"Oh, it's not dirt, just—"

"I never noticed it before," said Frankie, "but I like it. It makes you different. Unique."

On the way back to Lockwood (which seemed shorter than he remembered), Charles insisted that Frankie find a country station; and so they listened as the DJ played her favorites: Loretta Lynn and Tammy Wynette, which were better than Charles expected. At one point, she rested her hand on his arm, although when he decided to take her hand in his, she moved ever so slightly away.

Charles drove slowly toward the porch-less, two-story house, in need of paint, where Frankie lived with Clyde, her mother, and her brother Scott who, after a stint in the army, was back at home. "This is good," she said about halfway down the block. After he had pulled the Fairlane to the edge of the gravel street, she leaned across the console and kissed him—not long, but also not short—on the lips. "'Bye, Charles," she said as she slid out the door. "Do you want to go out again?" he called after her, but she may not have heard.

On Monday, however, when he stopped by Fashion on the Square immediately after the last customer had left, she said that, yes, she would meet him later in the city park, where he surprised her with a picnic scrounged from his parents' refrigerator. Instead of sitting across the rough table, with its attached benches, Frankie took a seat next to him, their hips occasionally touching, backs to the empty playground, as they ate the hastily-prepared chicken sandwiches and talked about what they had done that day. Charles did not reveal that much of his day had been spent mentally replaying their dinner by the river—and that kiss.

On Friday, he once again borrowed his mother's car, feeling astonishing energy despite a hard week of cleaning up after the storm. Once he had picked up Frankie on the west side of the square, they bought tenderloins, without onions, at the café-cum-grocery store in Martinsville (Frankie insisting that she pay), and drove to Lake Winyan. Charles steered the Fairlane to a secluded parking area on the east side of the lake, away from the lodge and the boat docks, where they made out, at first tentatively, then passionately. But just as Charles was beginning to wonder if the condom was really still in his wallet, Frankie said that Clyde had been feeling sick when she left, and she needed to get home so her mother could get some rest.

The following Monday, he lingered in the garage, making sure not to attract Clyde's attention and possible questions, so he would reach Fashion on the Square just before 5:00. After Frankie locked the door and turned the sign from "open" to "closed," they sat in the back, talking and kissing. On Tuesday, Jerry asked if Charles wanted to go with him to Don's, and he

122

considered asking Frankie if she wanted to come along, but thought better of it. Instead, he asked her to wait in the shop while he picked up cheeseburgers and Cokes at the Dairy Queen. "I like eating where it's not so noisy," he told her.

Frankie had let him know she was busy on Wednesday, so Charles was home when Randall, Cliff, and Kenny stopped by. They knew he'd been too worn out to ride around, said Randall with a grin, emphasizing "worn out," but maybe he'd like to go with them to St. Louis that weekend to see the Cardinals play the Cubs. "It looks like on Sunday the pitchers will be Gibson and Jenkins. Doesn't get any better than that!" They were going to stay, as the four of them had last year, at the Holiday Inn by the airport, with its pool and putting green. Charles tried to sound enthusiastic before telling them that, unfortunately, he already had plans. "A man of mystery," said Randall. "As if everyone doesn't know," said Cliff. At which point, his father showed up on the porch and greeted the three boys warmly.

"If your plans get changed," Randall called out from the sidewalk, "we'll need to know by tomorrow. After that, we'll ask Andy, now that the cast is off his arm, or somebody."

"Maybe we'll ask Nancy," said Cliff. "I hear she's free," which the three of them obviously found hilarious.

"Let's go sit on the patio," said his father, and when they got there, on the backside of the spacious house, Charles saw that a pitcher of iced tea and two glasses were already on the wicker table. Once they had each poured a glass, his father said, "So, you're not going to St. Louis this year? I thought you really enjoyed that."

"That's what I used to do," said Charles. "It's like people in this town want me to stay a kid."

"Is that why you're not playing any golf, either?" Charles shrugged his shoulders, and they sat quietly for a minute, shooing flies and swatting at the occasional mosquito. Finally, his father shifted loudly in his chair before saying, "Your mother and I thought we'd go to the lake this weekend, stay in the lodge. We've hardly had the boat out all summer. Maybe you could join us when you're through on Saturday, especially since you're not going to St. Louis. Or maybe Clyde will let you skip a Saturday. I've done him a few favors over—"

"Dad, come on! Stay out of my work. I don't want you talking to Clyde about doing me favors. On Saturdays, I pick up stuff with Moss. Some of it, by the way, he says is perfectly good stuff that you throw away."

"You know by now, I assume, that much of what Moss says is . . . well, it wouldn't hold up in court." He chuckled at his own phrasing.

"I like him."

"Well yes, he can be likable, if you can tune out the bluster. Like telling people he was a school teacher. Even at the school out by Stiles, he was a fill-in. Basically, he worked on his parents' farm until they had to sell it."

124

Charles slid his chair back and got up. "By the way," said his father, "I was on the city council when it was decided the street crew should work on Saturday mornings." Before Charles could speak, he added, "You can roll your eyes all you want, but you should know I voted for it because that was the only way Clarence the banker would agree to even slightly higher salaries for Clyde and the others. I know for sure that at least three of us on the council weren't thinking the crew should do much work on Saturdays. It was just what we had to do politically."

Charles stared at him before saying, "I've got things I need to do."

"Okay, but think about Saturday. We've invited the Harrises, and their niece is visiting from Ohio. She goes to Oberlin, and your mother and I—" But Charles was already headed to the back door and pretended not to hear.

Surprisingly, at least to Charles, Frankie told him on Friday (too late for Randall and company) that she would be tied up all weekend at a church revival.

"Really? Really?! What church do you go to?"

"It's my parents' church, Hope of the World Pentecostal Fellowship."

"Clyde is a Pentecostal?!"

"And so am I, Charles. What's so wrong with that? We don't have horns or three eyes."

He shook his head. "I didn't mean there's anything wrong with it." And when she didn't respond, he added, "I've never even seen that church."

"It's not in Lockwood," said Frankie. "It's on the road just as you're coming into West Valley. But I don't imagine you pay attention to little country churches."

The only person Charles talked to about Frankie was Jerry, making sure not to imply too much emotional investment, especially after Jerry, in the same breath, said, "That's great you're seeing her!" and asked, "Are you sure it's a good idea?" So on Monday, when Jerry wanted to know why he seemed so down in the dumps, Charles blurted out the story of the revival and how he hadn't seen Frankie all weekend. Sandy's out of town, somewhere with her sister, said Jerry, so I can let you have the Camaro for the evening. "I can guarantee," he said as he tossed Charles the keys, "that the back seat is big enough."

Having checked his wallet, twice, Charles picked up Frankie at the usual place. "I hope you haven't eaten," he said, as they headed down the Stringville Road toward Missouri. But while he had been hoping for another romantic evening, he realized as they pulled into the parking lot that Don's Café and Tavern wasn't the right place for it, especially since Frankie had been more reserved than usual ever since he picked her up in the Camaro, and she seemed to sigh deeply as he opened her door. He asked her, twice, if anything was wrong. "Is this place okay?"

126

"Why do you keep asking me that? Just say what you want to do, and if I really don't want to do it, I'll tell you."

"I just want to make sure—"

"Charles, you worry way too much! I'm not high maintenance, okay? Not like Nancy Johnston or whoever else you used to take out."

Once inside, she moved quickly to a booth, and then spent time studying the menu pressed against the wall by plastic ketchup and mustard bottles. She even read the menu's back cover with all its advertisements for businesses in Lancaster and Lockwood, including the West Side Café and the pool hall. When the waitress (not Sandy) finally arrived, Charles ordered a beer, Frankie a Coke, even though he assured her she could drink alcohol here despite being only twenty.

"Charles, I know how old I am."

What to talk about? Finally, he asked, "What went on at the revival?"

"It's hard to explain. You kind of have to be there." He persisted until she said, "There is a lot of singing and praying, and we had an evangelist who preached about hope, I guess because of our name."

And so he asked her, "What do *you* hope for?"

She smiled for the first time that evening. "I'd like a raise."

"No, really—"

"Yes, really. I would like a raise so I can get a place of my own, get out of Clyde's house. I've slept in the same awful, claustrophobic bedroom, with the same wallpaper and the same bedspread, for twenty years!"

Her vehemence caught him off guard. "I get it," he said at last. "Going away to Drake gets me out . . . but I mean, beyond all that. When you think of the longer future—"

She interrupted him. "Why are you asking all this?"

"I just want to know you better. Like why you didn't go to college. You're smart. You could've gone —"

She cut him off again. "On whose dollar? It costs money to keep going to school, Charles, and I wasn't blessed that way, was I?" When he was quiet, she said, "Okay, I always wanted to dance. Not just like a high school dance, but real dance. That's not going to happen. So what do I hope for? I hope someday I can see a ballet, a real ballet." She took a sip of the Coke. "Okay, what about you?"

So Charles talked about his hope—expectation, really—of going to graduate school, although he wasn't sure of his focus. Probably history of some sort. Then he talked about his hope—expectation—of going to Paris, of sitting in sidewalk cafés where he can use his French. Maybe live in Paris someday. His mother's name, Madeleine, is French, and maybe because of her he has always had a desire to spend time there. He began to describe the pictures his parents brought back from their recent trip to Strasbourg and the Alsace region, an area he was sure he would visit, when he noticed Frankie smiling. "Does this sound pretty silly?"

128

She shook her head. "I just don't think I can think that big. The farthest I ever traveled is when we all went to the Black Hills."

"Well, of course I don't know if—"

"Does getting married, having babies, figure in these big plans?"

"Yeah, sure, at some point, I guess."

Their food had arrived, but Frankie, who had barely touched hers, sat looking down at her plate. She took a deep breath. "Charles, why did you ask me out? If it's just to have a good time for a month or two . . . fine. That's what it is. But I have a feeling you started talking to me because I'm Clyde's daughter."

"No, Frankie. I like you . . . a lot."

"Charles, you're sweet. But we don't have anything, at least not much, in common."

"That's not true!"

"In high school, we had three classes together. I bet you didn't know that, did you? We were in Mr. Bartholomew's history class together, but I could tell that first night you didn't remember it. You were the star—Charles Weaver, the smartest kid in the class, in the school. I don't think you even looked at a B student, a B- student, like me. So now I'm supposed to believe that I'm something special to you?"

They sat, picking at their food in silence, until Frankie reached across the table and took his hand. "I'm sorry, Charles. I like going out with you. I like hearing you talk about your plans.

And, like I said, it is what it is. But," she squeezed his hand, "don't expect me to be something I'm not. Okay? And don't expect me to spread my legs in the back of Jerry Hinkle's sexmobile. Why'd you have to borrow that car, anyway?"

However, when they got to the Camaro, with no one parked near them in a corner of the lot, she quickly unbuttoned her blouse and welcomed his hands to places they had never been, until he tried to go further, and she suggested they head back up Stringville Road. Just stay out of the ditch, she told him.

On Thursday morning (for years after, Charles would remember that it was the 3rd of August), there was an unusual swarm of activity around the city office, next door to the street crew's garage. Clyde didn't limp into the garage until after 8:00, and when he did, it was with big news. Last night, the Mars Hill Church had pretty much burned to the ground. Reports were that only two of the walls were standing, and only part of them. "Woody thinks it was druggies, prob'ly broke in to use it for cookin' up meth—that what they call it?—and then it blew up. Woody asked the state boys to clean up the mess at the church, but they're working on that bridge worshed out in the storm out by West Valley, so they wanta know if we'll do it. I told 'em we prob'ly could." He smiled. "Long as they keep loanin' us that tar spreader."

"If it's a crime scene," said Jerry, "*should* it be cleaned up?"

"I said the same thing, but Woody 'parently told 'em he'll do all the investigatin' that needs doin' today, so I want you and Charlie to go up there first thing in the morning. It may take you a couple of days." He looked at Charles with a smile. "But after dealin' with that mess tomorrow, you can sleep in on Saturday, let Moss make his run 'round the square by hisself for a change."

That evening, Charles' father, who was a member of the Mars Hill Preservation Committee, was both despondent and furious. "The oldest log church in the whole state. No nails in it, just fitted together with wooden pins, or used to be. I hope to hell Woody catches them." When Charles told him that he was on clean-up duty, his father said, "See if there are any logs that can be reused, maybe set them aside, because we sure as hell are going to rebuild it."

Although both had grown up in Savannah County, neither Charles nor Jerry had ever been to the old church, buried as it is in the hills near the river. Clyde gave them directions: Highway 19 north to what people call the Turner Road, which is about a half mile past the gas station, then east to the second or, maybe, third road to the north—the one by the old Pettit place. Perhaps, said Moss tentatively, they should go through Florence, which was a bit out of the way, but on slightly better roads. "Nah," said Clyde. "Go the way I told ya, the second or third road to the north, then to the right up the biggest hill in the county."

Of course they got lost. They went back to the gas station on Highway 19, where the owner told them it is the fourth road

131

going north. Back to what they assumed was the Turner Road turnoff, then to the fourth gravel road, which was partially hidden by a huge tree and a dilapidated house, now the color of the earth around it. "The Pettits don't look very prosperous," said Jerry, as they made the turn. They crossed a bridge with a sign that read "Impassible in High Water," then jogged right at a fork in the road, until that way ended at a lane marked "Privat! No Truspassers! That means U!" Back to the fork, where this time they went left, passing between small cornfields, then a curve to the right past a solitary farmhouse and up the heavily-wooded hill, the road so rutted that the old pickup shimmied even though they were going no more than twenty-five. They had been talking about college and Clyde and the Cardinals and Frankie and Sandy, but now, as the road curved left, then right, then left, they just stared out the windows, the landscape occasionally unfolding beneath them in a scene Charles vowed to remember.

And then, there it was. The white sign that identified it as "Mars Hill Church (1857)"—carefully, but unprofessionally, lettered—standing about twenty yards from the burned-out, one-room structure. Only one complete wall was left standing, and even the planks that formed a ramp to the door were charred. To the left, as they faced the remnants of the church, were the gravel road and the valley beyond. To the right was a heavy stand of trees, and, in front of it, a small cemetery. There was also a clearing beneath the trees where two or three cars could park. After unloading their tools—brooms, shovels, rakes, and a wheelbarrow—they wandered through the cemetery, peering at barely legible markers from the mid-nineteenth century. Charles, the history-major-to-be, said, "I wish I'd come here before now," and Jerry agreed.

Eventually, they got to work. Jerry brought a transistor radio, but, despite being on a hill, the reception was poor, so they worked mostly in silence, almost as if there were a holiness to the place that infected them. They started by moving the larger logs, stacking the reusable ones in one pile, the destroyed ones in another. Two backless pews had survived, and these they moved to a separate place near the sign. The sun was hot, but a breeze made it almost pleasant.

Clyde had instructed them to clear out what remained of the church so that the committee, or whoever, could decide whether rebuilding with some of the old logs was a realistic option. "You're good with a broom and a rake," he said to Charles. "Sweep it up, dump the ash somewhere. See what's left to work with." So, after a quick stop for lunch, they began the laborious task of sweeping the ash and splinters into piles, shoveling the piles into the wheelbarrow, and dumping it among the trees. There didn't seem to be any drug paraphernalia in the mess. "I guess," said Jerry, "Woody must of picked up all that stuff."

The church was surrounded by about eight feet of cleared ground, much of it covered in gravel, which may have kept the surrounding trees from burning but made the wheelbarrow harder to push. Mercifully, beyond the gravel there was the hint

133

of a path where the weeds were flattened between the trees, which at least made it less difficult to cart away the debris. Midway through the afternoon the wind picked up, and the ash began to blow, until Charles and Jerry were more gray than flesh-colored, and they wished they had Clyde's scratched-up goggles.

With about an hour to go, they took a break, passing the thermos back and forth. And when they resumed, it was Charles' turn on the wheelbarrow. As he strained to push it over the weedy, bumpy terrain, he tried to think of the Cardinals, French verbs, Paris cafés, but always his mind came back to Frankie—in the restaurant, by the lake, in the Camaro. He tried to remember if he had ever been this excited about being with Nancy.

Since the ground near the edge of the trees was already covered in ash and chunks of charred wood, he ventured farther, then farther still. Nothing could be better for building muscles, he told himself, than pushing a loaded wheelbarrow. Ahead of him—quite a ways ahead, as it turned out—was a large, moss-covered rock where, with every muscle aching, he decided he could rest and think about Frankie, before trudging back for a final load or two.

And it was there he saw it. First just an arm, burned so black it could be mistaken for a branch. But as he rounded the rock, he was hit by the smell, like the time his mother had burned liver on the stove, and then by the sight of the insect-covered torso and the face, the skin stretched and shiny, already beginning to decompose.

Chapter Seven

Lockwood has a local newspaper that is published twice a week, under different names. On Tuesday, it is the *Lockwood Democrat*, on Friday, the *Lockwood Republican*. Charles was convinced his mother read it more intensely on Tuesdays, his father on Fridays. But that may simply have reflected how he read his parents.

On Monday, August 7, the paper published a special edition, complete with large photographs of Charles, Jerry, and Sheriff Wood on the front page, and soon it seemed the whole town was buzzing with the news. There was even mention of it in the *Des Moines Register*. Neither paper, Charles' mother pointed out, bothered to mention that he was high school valedictorian.

According to the sheriff, the body was not yet identified, but it certainly was not someone from Savannah County. "Outsiders come in thinking they can hide in the countryside. It doesn't look like anyone local was involved." This didn't make much sense to Charles. Why would someone not from around there decide to mix drugs in an old church that is even difficult for locals to find? How would they know about it, or know that it's not in use unless someone local told them? Charles said something to that effect when Jack, the local reporter, interviewed him at home the day after he found the body.

This, however, was only the second of four interviews. The first came from Connie who woke him up on Saturday (the one Saturday he could sleep in) to learn all the gory details.

"How do *you* know I found a body?"

"It's Lockwood, Charles. The whole town knows. Or at least the people who actually talk to other people know. Julie heard it from . . . It doesn't matter! How did you find the body? What did it look like?!"

Reluctantly sitting up in bed, he told her the story, emphasizing the maggots and pus, until she interrupted him. "Why didn't you come home last night and tell us about it? Mom wasn't sure whether to save some dinner for you or not."

"For your information, I called Mom and told her what I was doing."

"Why doesn't anybody tell me these things?"

"I thought you knew everything that's going on in Lockwood."

She made a face at him. "So what did you tell Mom?"

"That we had to report what we found to the sheriff's office. Not Woody, he was gone somewhere, but Tim. That took a long time, because Mildred in the office had to call him on the radio. And then I met a friend."

"You mean you had a date with Frankie."

"How do you know who I have a date with?"

"Charles, everybody knows you're going out with Frankie, although nobody can figure out why. Well, they know why." She grinned widely while raising her eyebrows.

"You're crazy. Go away!"

Connie stopped leaning on his dresser and headed for the door. "Charles," she said as she was leaving, "everybody knows about Frankie, except maybe you."

In fact, he and Frankie had spent barely an hour together on Friday evening, enough time to share a Grape Nehi in the city park, and for her to tell him she was tied up with family the rest of the weekend. Charles, of course, was bubbling over with his news; but Frankie—while she listened, as always, intently— asked surprisingly few questions. And her comments were mainly about how awful it would be to burn to death, a point Charles had failed to mention in his narration of the day's events or to think much about.

His father was out of town for a lawyers' conference in Des Moines, spending an extra day, at his wife's insistence, with his sister-in-law, Aunt Gloria; but Charles' mother found him as soon as he returned from talking with Jack, the local reporter. "Were you going to tell me about your adventure?"

139

"I told you pretty much everything over the phone last night. We were cleaning up the church and found the body of someone who got burned in the fire. Not much more to tell."

"I think there is, like how you're feeling about it. It's traumatic to stumble upon a dead body, especially a burned one. I can only imagine what that looks like, or smells like." She scrunched up her face. "I'm surprised you could sleep last night."

Charles realized he had been more disturbed by the prospect of not seeing Frankie over the weekend than by images of the charred body, but kept that to himself. He shrugged, then seeing his mother was expecting more, added, "I'm okay. After I found it, and after Jerry saw it, we drove to the farmhouse along the road to the church to see if we could use their phone. But nobody answered when we knocked, so we just drove back to Lockwood to try and find the sheriff. We didn't spend much time looking at the body; it all happened so fast, we didn't have time to think too much about what it looked like." When his mother didn't respond, Charles asked, "Have you told Dad?"

"Yes, I spoke to him last night. He has some crazy notion there is bad karma in that corner of the county, since this is close to where that farmer and his wife were killed."

"I thought—"

"I'm sure," she continued, "your father will want to hear all about it when he gets back on Monday. So please don't make other plans for after dinner."

140

Since Charles skipped Sunday worship, where people were bound to have lots of questions, the final interview came on Monday. He had just entered the city garage, Jerry not thirty seconds behind him, when Clyde announced that Woody wanted to see them. They were to meet him in the conference room in the courthouse. How soon? Now.

Charles had expected to meet with the sheriff at some point, and had rehearsed the details in his mind: how they had started sweeping up the ashes and small debris, loading it all in the wheelbarrow and spreading it among the trees; how he happened, almost by accident, to look behind the rock; how they reported immediately what they had found.

The interview, however, turned out to be more of an interrogation. Without speaking, the sheriff led them to a ground-floor room with elongated windows and motioned for them to sit near the end of a long, oak conference table. He remained standing. "Clyde sent you out to Mars Hill?" It was as much a statement as a question.

Jerry said nothing, so Charles answered: "He said you asked the street crew to clean up after the fire."

"No," the tone sarcastic, "I asked the state crew to clean it up."

"Doesn't your nephew work for them?" Jerry's tone was equally sarcastic, and for several seconds the sheriff simply stared at him.

"That's why I knew *they* would do a good job of it."

141

Jerry looked like he was going to reply, but then hesitated, and the sheriff turned his attention to Charles. "Why were you so far from the church? I bet your orders was just to clean up the building site."

"I was dumping ashes. We were trying to spread out the debris so it—"

"There are lots of places where you could have dumped those ashes. Why were you way out in *that* spot?"

"It wasn't *that* far into the trees," said Jerry, with a forcefulness that made Charles feel good. "Why are you asking about this? We were just doing what we were told to do."

"I went that direction," said Charles, "because there was a kind of path where the weeds were all bent down, or kind of bent down. Looking back on it, I'd say the body was probably dragged—"

"Oh, so now you're Sherlock Holmes." As Charles turned to see how Jerry was reacting, the sheriff shouted, "Look at me when I'm talking to you! I don't need a couple of kids telling me how to do my job or second guessing me in the newspaper."

"What are you talking about?" asked Jerry, who obviously hadn't seen the special edition. The sheriff pulled a copy from his hip pocket and slid it across the table.

"Little Sherlock here contradicts what I said about the investigation, as if he knows shit about what I've discovered."

"How," asked Jerry, "would he know what you said to Jack about the investigation?"

142

"One side of the body was covered in mud or ashes or something," Charles continued. "At least it seemed to be when I saw it, and Jerry saw it, too. So it seems to me the body was dragged, which means someone else was there. I just said I thought it must be, or could be, someone from around here because Mars Hill is so out of the way. You'd have to know how to get there. That's all I said."

By the time they got back to the garage, the other three were gone, along with the pickup. They checked in the city office to see if Clyde had left them any instructions, but he hadn't, so they plopped on the couch, growing increasingly agitated as they replayed the "interview." The sheriff had finally asked what Charles had seen when he first looked around the rock, but why had he asked if they had moved the body? Who would want to touch *that* if they didn't have to? Was he suggesting they had searched it? Why in the world would they do that?

When the others returned a little before noon, Clyde, his leg still in a splint, was in a somber mood. "I sure didn't expect to get you boys knee-deep in some investigation."

"Are they calling it suspicious?" asked Moss.

"Well, 'course it's suspicious," said Clyde in an irritated tone. "Some stranger found dead and burned up in the middle a nowhere . . . 'course it's suspicious. But if you're suggestin' it's a murder, you been readin' too much of that Shakespeare. Paper made it sound like drugs was involved. Some idiot blew hisself up mixing whatever they call it."

143

So Charles told about the bent-down weeds and the mud or ashes on the body. Moss asked questions while Clyde and Dexter sat silently smoking in their usual places. Finally, Jerry cut in. "The point is that Woody's not taking any of this seriously. You should've heard what he asked us in the courthouse! He was a lot more concerned to cover his ass because *he* didn't look far enough in the woods than he was to find out what we saw, what Charles saw."

Clyde nodded, poking at the tobacco in his pipe bowl with the wood end of a match. After a long pause, he said, "Yep, he can get purdy defensive. He's way too hard on Moss here, maybe 'cause of somethin' he thinks he remembers from high school," a comment that made Moss smile and nod. "But he's not a bad person, not any more so than the rest of us." He relit his pipe, shook out the match and tossed it on the floor. "You know Miss Sadie, lives over the café?" Without waiting for a reply, he continued: "Woody takes food up those rickety stairs every day. Ain't that right, Dexter?"

Dexter nodded and rocked. "Pert near. Far's I can tell."

"Usually gets somethin' after Ginny closes, and takes it up to her."

"Why does he do that?" asked Jerry.

"You have to ask him. But I 'spect it has somethin' to do with him growin' up in that apartment over the hardware store where the Thompson woman lives."

Moss started to say, "We picked up a sack of her—"

144

Clyde cut him off. "And he's mad as a wet hen that some lawyer's tryin' to get Miss Sadie evicted."

Charles stopped by Fashion on the Square at 5:00, mainly to tell Frankie he needed to be home that evening. She seemed less disappointed than he would have wished, but they did manage a kiss—a fine, long kiss—in the back room. She also told him that she sometimes got coffee mid-morning at the 7-Eleven a block north of the square, a fact that Charles filed away for future reference.

After supper that evening, both father and son seemed anxious to make their way to the study, where they settled on either side of the big mahogany desk. On the walls around them hung historic photographs of Lockwood, including one of the courthouse lawn surrounded by a railing, where horses were tied, and one of the train depot before it was torn down. Charles' father clearly wanted to talk about the Mars Hill Church; but while others had been focused on the body, his father wanted to know if Charles and Jerry had saved many logs and benches that could be used in the rebuilding.

Charles, however, had other topics in mind, and his father sat quietly while he railed about the meeting with the sheriff. "What difference does it make how far I was from the church? Even if Jerry and I were taking a break, which we weren't, what business is that of his? People should be asking why *he* didn't look all around the area. It wasn't *that* far! Even Jerry said so. And why would he think we touched the body?"

"Well, you want him to do his job," said his father. "Asking questions is his job. I don't see why that's so far out of line." After looking at Charles' face, he added, "But I'll admit that he can be a bastard sometimes, the way he goes about things. But other times he's not. Have you talked to your friend Randall lately?" Charles shook his head. "The story I hear is that Woody stopped him, I think it was just last weekend, driving under the influence." His father smiled. "Harry said he heard Randall was drunk as a skunk, but that may be a bit exaggerated. Anyway, Woody asked him where he was going, and when Randall said he was going home, Woody said, 'I know you are, because I'm going to follow you there.' Which he did without giving Randall a ticket or worse. So he can be a pretty good fellow at times."

"That's what people keep saying, but it's not what I see." It seemed as if his father was about to change the subject, probably back to logs and benches, so Charles brought up the other thing on his mind: "Are you the lawyer who's trying to evict Sadie, Miss Sadie, from her apartment on the square?"

His father stared at him, then smiled slightly and shook his head. "Who have you been talking to? This didn't come up in your conversation with the sheriff, did it?"

"*Are* you?"

A deep breath. "Connor, who owns the café and the building it's in, is within his legal rights. Mrs. Rayburn—Sadie—has been

146

renting from him . . . at a very cheap rate, I might add, for many years. And now he needs the space, and she refuses to move. So, yes, I am representing Connor."

"Where is she supposed to go?! She can't even get up and down those stairs."

"Well," said his father, "that's also part of the point, isn't it? It's not safe for her to be there. Think what would happen if there was a fire, which has happened on the square before, you know."

Charles sat back in his chair and looked down. "It just isn't fair," he said, but in a softer voice. "People like her and Dexter and Clyde—maybe not Clyde so much, but Moss—get pushed around, and it seems like you're on the side of those who do the pushing."

For the first time in the conversation, his father adopted his authoritative tone. "You seem to know all about it, Mister Stand-Up-For-the-Poor. But I guess no one's told you how I offered to pay, out of *my* pocket, for her transition to the nursing home, where she would be a hell of a lot better off than in an apartment over the café filled with cooking fumes. Right? And I've been looking for state money to keep her there." He paused. "Life's messy, Charles. I'm sorry I haven't made that clear to you before now." Another pause. "Although, from what I hear, you've managed to complicate your life quite a bit this summer."

Charles didn't like where this was heading, so raised a different grievance. "Why is everything *yours*?" Again, his

147

father seemed caught off guard, and Charles quickly continued. "You talk about money coming out of *your* pocket. Everybody calls this *your* house. Sometimes, it's like Mom isn't here or doesn't want to be here."

His father pursed his lips in the way Charles hated, but then it was as if the air went out of him, and he seemed to slump in his big swivel chair. "It hasn't always been easy for her, that's true." For some reason, Charles had an image of his father pausing to fiddle with a pipe, although he knew he didn't smoke. "Your mother wanted to live in Des Moines when I finished law school. I had an offer, so it was possible. But she wasn't attached there."

"Aunt Gloria's there."

"Yes, she's there, her sister is there, that's true. But their parents, as you know, had already moved to Ohio. And all of my roots are here." He looked out the window, slowly swiveling the chair, one way, then the other. "You know the Llewellyn place not too far north of Martinsville?" Charles wanted to say, *You've told me this a hundred times, and we've driven past it fifty,* but his father wasn't looking at him, and it didn't seem like a time to interrupt. "Your great-grandfather had a farm on one part—one corner, really—of their property. That's the old house." He pointed to another historic photograph behind his desk, the house so small it was dwarfed by two large trees. "This whole county feels to me . . . your mother, though, it's true, she has never loved it. Lockwood feels too . . . small for her. No right or

148

wrong, just how she feels. But then you and Connie came along, and we agreed—it wasn't just me, *we* agreed—that it wouldn't be good to leave." He swiveled until he was again facing Charles. "I don't know, maybe we should have, but we didn't. Every so often, we take these trips, mainly to France since that's her dream spot, but that only goes so far."

Neither of them spoke for what seemed to Charles like ten minutes, although it was probably only one. Finally, his father said, "Well, anyway, you'll be in Des Moines soon, and you'll need some way to get around. So I thought perhaps we could look at cars tomorrow after you get off work, unless you have other plans." He smiled. "Of course, it won't be a fancy Camaro, like your friend Jerry's."

"I don't want a fancy Camaro," said Charles.

On Tuesday, he again stopped by Fashion on the Square, this time as soon as he got off work, risking the presence of customers in order to tell Frankie about the car-buying excursion, which would mean another evening apart. She agreed it was for a good cause, and reminded him (as if he needed reminding) that she would be at church on Wednesday. So they agreed—in between customers, as he stood silently in the back room—to take a ride in his new car on Thursday. Maybe drive the eighteen miles to Mahaska and see a movie.

Jerry and Charles had planned to go to Don's Café on Wednesday, but once they were in the Camaro, Jerry told him

149

that Sandy was acting weird, so he would just as soon stay in Lockwood. "Let's go over to the pool hall. Ralph gives me a beer whenever I play pool. Nobody cares." Since they were already in the car, he drove the Camaro four hundred feet to the east side of the square and pulled into a diagonal spot facing the pool hall. As he was getting out of the car, Charles saw a book, *Basic French Grammar*, on the back seat and started to say, "Did I . . ." when he realized it wasn't his. When he looked up, Jerry was smiling.

Several men were in the pool hall: three at the bar, beneath a sign reading "Where There's Life, There's Bud"; three more playing pool in the back half of the large, smoky room; and Henry of the garbage crew's son, Hank, sitting by the front window, his bad leg stretched out on a chair in front of him. "Lookie here," he said as Jerry and Charles pushed open the swinging door, "it's the boys from the street crew. Ralph, you better give these boys somethin' to drink. They been workin' up a sweat wastin' taxpayers' dollars."

"What you know about payin' taxes?" said a loud man at the bar, and all the men in the front of the room laughed.

"I'll pour you two a beer," said Ralph, from behind the bar. "Just put it on the floor if Woody comes in."

"He's got better things to do, don't he?" said the loud man, loudly. "Drugheads in our county blowin' themselves up. What's he care about a beer or two?"

150

They took their glasses to a table away from the bar, Charles wiping off the spills and crumbs with the back of his hand. "I bet you wouldn't have done that in May," said Jerry with a big smile.

"What's the deal with Sandy?"

"It's nothing. I'm going back to Iowa City, she's moving on. It's what happens."

"There's something," said Charles, "I've been wanting to ask." He paused while the men in the back whooped over a well-played shot. "Does Sandy know Frankie? I raised the idea of a double date with you and Sandy, and Frankie just laughed and then got really quiet. Didn't say no, just laughed and changed the subject, which she's really good at. Was she the friend who set you up with Sandy at the beginning of the summer?"

Jerry took a long drink, finishing off his beer. "Yeah, she knew her from some place. Lancaster's not that far."

"So . . . are you a . . . good friend of Frankie's?"

"You know," said Jerry, "that we were in the same grade." Pause. "Why don't you just ask me if I had sex with her? That's what you want to know, isn't it?" When Charles didn't answer, Jerry continued: "The answer is no, I didn't, I haven't. There wouldn't have been any . . ."

"Any what?"

"She was going out with some guy most of the time."

"When did that stop? Who was it?"

"You think I remember who Frankie went out with? I think they were mostly farmers."

"They?!"

"Come on, Charles. She's not a nun or something." He rubbed his fingers up and down the empty glass. "I like Frankie. She's a friend, and she's a good person who likes to have fun, like anybody."

"When did you get the Camaro?"

Jerry smiled and shook his head. "At the beginning of last summer. Why do you want to know that?"

"Did you take Frankie out last—"

"Look, I told you we went out once, maybe twice. It didn't go anywhere, okay? We just decided to stay friends."

Two men had entered the hall, and Charles and Jerry were quiet while they passed on their way to a pool table. It was Jerry who picked up the conversation. "When I warned you about seeing her—"

"You didn't *warn* me. When did you warn me?"

"Okay, when I asked you if it was a good idea, it wasn't because of who she is, but because of whose daughter she is." He leaned across the table and said in a softer voice, "You want to know the real reason I'm here this summer? My mom acts like she has money, helping me buy that car and all, but she doesn't. Not really. So, when I didn't get a basketball scholarship, I took a job during the school year at a Herman's sporting goods. Anyway, the manager's daughter worked there, too, and we got together a few times. Not a big deal. Sort of like with Sandy. But he found out and got really pissed off."

"Who did?"

"The manager, her dad. He didn't just fire me. Said he was going to tell the university, whatever that might mean. That's when I decided it would be better to come home for the summer, work here. *Et voila! Je suis ici.* So the moral of the story is be careful. We know you're not serious about Frankie. Clyde knows you're not serious about Frankie. And you know how he gets sometimes." He smiled. "But for now, just go with it. It's been a summer of love!"

Jerry went to the bar for two more beers, and when he came back, he asked, "So, have you and Frankie done it yet? That's the real question." Charles started to nod, sort of, and Jerry continued. "Well, if you haven't, it's probably because Frankie's not clear whether you're serious about Frankie. For Sandy, I'm just a guy to have fun with. I mean she likes me, but it's not serious. Frankie must think it could be more than that. Or at least she wants it to be."

"What," Charles asked, "does that have to do with having sex?"

Jerry shook his head. "I know I don't understand women, but, man, you really don't have a clue."

The tone of their conversation lightened. They gleefully relived the time a woman stepped over their caution tape, right into the middle of the cement they had just poured and smoothed in front of the grade school—and then kept on walking, like it was nothing! Jerry was laughing so hard he nearly spilled his beer. "How could she not know she was walking in wet cement? What a ditz!"

They repeated stories Clyde had told them, including one about a man who ran into a Stop sign and then blamed Clyde and Dexter for putting it too near the street. But since others were staring at them, they reduced the volume of their laughter. They started to talk about the man in a car with Missouri plates who stopped to ask them for directions to the Methodist Church, when they were standing not fifteen feet from the sign reading, "Savannah County Methodist Church," but suddenly all talk was interrupted by a familiar voice, coming from just inside the swinging door. "Any of you layabouts know who owns this fancy red car out front, with the fancy racing stripes? It looks to me like the Hinkle kid's, but he's not old enough to be in here drinkin', is he Ralph?"

"Now Woody," said the man at the bar, less loudly, "they're not hurtin' nobody."

"Next," said the sheriff, "you are gonna be tellin' me they're good workers." There was laughter around the room, but nervous. "Don't look so glum, Ralph. I'm not here to bust you, at least not for this." More laughter. "What I want to know is if you've seen any out-of-towners, the kind that would hang out in a dump like this."

154

When no one responded, Hank said, "From what I hear, there's one less of 'em after last Friday." Subdued laughter.

"Although, from what I read," said the man at the bar, "these boys over here," he gestured at Charles and Jerry, "think there might be someone from around Lockwood involved."

When the sheriff next spoke, any levity was gone from his voice. "These boys," he said, addressing the whole room, "go off to take a piss, or whatever they were doin' way out in the woods, stumble over the remains of some druggie nobody gives a damn about, and now they think they're big-time detectives. I think they've been watchin' too much 'Dragnet' and—what's this new one?—'Colombo.' All they need's a trench coat." More laughter, but again with a nervous edge. "Suggestin' things to Jack, instead of leaving it to people who know what they're doing."

"But Woody," said the man at the bar, "at least they found the body. No telling how long it would have been there if—"

"Ralph," said the sheriff abruptly, "Ernie here's had enough. It's clouding his judgment." No laughter. Again he spoke to the room. "You all know I keep things under control in this county. Have a few beers, who cares. But I know what goes on. Am I right?" A few nods. The sheriff stomped his foot loudly. "Am I right?!" More vigorous nodding. "Like I know these boys drive to Missoura to drink, even know how they ran that fancy car in the ditch one night."

Charles and Jerry left the pool hall not long after the sheriff. They didn't speculate on how he knew about their near accident, and Charles didn't bother to tell his father about the encounter.

Charles' times with Frankie had settled into a pattern with lots of kissing and touching, but not all the way, and not on Wednesdays—all made easier now that he had a car of his own. He would have preferred something small and sporty, like the used Mustang they looked at briefly in Mahaska. But his father who, afterall, was paying, insisted on something bigger and safer. "This is mainly for trips to and from Des Moines, so it needs to be safe on the highway," as if, Charles said to himself, this used Buick would protect him from the semis that barreled along Iowa highways. If his grandfather had been driving a Mustang, he might have been able to speed out of the way. Still, it was a car.

Charles and Frankie also talked in a way that he had never experienced. She claimed not to read a newspaper, and yet he found that she knew all about the riots in Newark and Detroit and Milwaukee. "If I grew up there," said Frankie, "I'd probably be rioting, too." Why, Charles wondered, did he find that surprising?

They talked about sports. She liked baseball (a Cardinals fan, of course), but not wrestling . . . or golf. They talked about people they knew, including her friend, Callie Moss, who had had two backroom abortions.

156

"Does Moss know this?" Charles asked.

"I don't know. But you sure won't be the one to tell him, or you've seen the last of me!"

They talked about popular music. Charles discovered that Frankie, while claiming to be a fan only of country, knew all the words to "Light My Fire" and "Purple Haze" and "Ruby Tuesday" and "Happy Together." He couldn't say the same, he realized, about "I Fall to Pieces" or "You Ain't Woman Enough."

They talked about clothes and how Frankie thought it was silly the way women's fashions changed every year—every season, for God's sake!

"I guess it gives you a job. I guess it gives a lot of people jobs, making all those new clothes."

"I suppose," said Frankie, "but it also makes people spend money they don't have. The other day I tried to talk Wendy Slaughter out of buying one of these new miniskirts in some ridiculous color just because she saw one like it on television. I knew she couldn't afford it, working at Dairy Queen, but she had to have it. No changing *her* mind."

Charles really wanted to ask why Frankie didn't dress at least a little more fashionably. At work she looked okay, but, once she was off the square, fashion was definitely not her thing. Surely she got an employee discount. And it would be easier to consider having a meal with his parents if she looked a little less . . . country or . . . dowdy. Such thoughts, however, went unsaid.

They talked about Lockwood and whether there would even be stores such as Fashion on the Square in twenty years. "My dad thinks the town is dying," Charles told her. "Pretty soon, he says, it'll just be a bedroom community for Mahaska." He smiled. "Of course, my mother says it's no wonder no one wants to live in a place like this."

"But people *do* want to live here," said Frankie. "It's just that the people here don't like the ones who are coming. That's what Reverend Miller says. They don't want the Amish. They don't want Negros or Mexicans. He says that's a sure way for the town not to grow."

Frankie talked about her mother. "I'm a lot like her, in some ways, although I don't look much like her and she's never worked, except at home, of course. I can always talk with her about things, and it's like she knows what's on my mind before I say it." Charles tried to gauge how much he could ask without giving away that the only time he'd seen Frankie's mother was when they took Clyde to the hospital, and that he might not know her if he saw her on the street.

Charles wanted Frankie to talk more about herself, but she usually deflected those conversations, often by asking about him. Sitting at a table in the otherwise deserted city park, she responded to a question about the scar on her wrist by asking, "Haven't any hard things happened to you?"

"My grandparents being crushed by a semi was pretty hard."

For the first time Charles could recall, Frankie blushed. She looked down and nodded. "Of course. I'm sorry I said that. Of course, everyone has hard things." She paused. "It's just that your life is . . . Sorry."

"What were you going to say? My life is what?"

"I was wrong, okay?" When Charles was silent, she finally added, "Things seem so easy for you, Charles. Like school. Did you ever get a B? Did you ever, I don't know, get really in trouble, do something really stupid? Did your dad ever—"

"Did he ever what?" It was clear, however, that Frankie had said all she was going to say on the subject.

But they did talk about Clyde, sort of. They were sitting in the new (used) car, drinking milkshakes, when Charles asked, "Does your dad have some kind of major illness?"

Frankie stared at him before looking down. "Why are you asking that?"

"I don't know. He just hasn't seemed 'right' since the sand spreader fell on his leg. Maybe before that. Yeah, even before that. He's been—"

"Clyde's tough," said Frankie. "He'll get through it."

"Get through what?" When she didn't answer but, instead, made a loud, sucking sound with her straw, Charles decided to ask another question: "Is it true he hit you that time you showed up at school with a black eye and your face all swollen?"

Frankie smiled and exhaled sharply. "So you did notice me, at least when I had a black eye and looked terrible. Did you and your crowd make fun of how I looked?"

"No, no! We wouldn't do anything like that."

"Charles, is that why we're going out, so you can pump me for information about Clyde?"

"No, Frankie! Really! I just . . . he has this reputation, and he does get angry. But at other people, not so much at me. And I just wondered if he got that way with you."

Again, Frankie looked at him intently (those eyes!), with a slight smile. "You don't get it, do you? Clyde likes you because you aren't like us, me and my brothers, or like him. He sees something different in you. Of course, if you were his son, he would think you weren't tough enough; but since you aren't, he likes how you are."

"Did he tell you that?"

Now Frankie laughed out loud. "We don't talk about things like that. I can just tell." She paused. "Charles, you're a really nice guy. You're not stuck up like you could be, like I thought you were. You've just got a lot of things to learn, and he thinks you'll learn them, somewhere away from here." She stirred the shake with her straw, and they sat silently while the radio played The Supremes.

Finally, Charles said, "I guess he knows we're dating."

She nodded. "I imagine he does. Not much happens in Lockwood Clyde doesn't know about."

160

"You haven't talked with him about it? I mean, he hasn't said anything to me, but I thought he might to you."

"It's come up, kind of 'round about."

"What does he—?"

"I don't know! Does it matter? I imagine he doesn't like it much because he thinks I'll get hurt. But, then, Clyde thinks getting hurt is just how things are." She stirred some more. "He's stood with me through some pretty bad times," something Charles both wanted, and didn't want, to ask about.

They finished their shakes before he did ask, "What does your brother think of us going out?"

"He thinks I'm stupid going around with a smart guy like you." That smile.

"He hasn't talked to me about it, although I guess I've never talked to him about much of anything."

"And he won't either. Scott's always saying how he's watching out for me, but Clyde told him to mind his own business and not be bothering either one of us. That much I do know. Why are you asking all these questions?"

"I just want to know more about who you are. There are whole parts of your life, like Wednesday evenings, that I don't know anything about."

"Then come with me," she said, "this Wednesday."

And thus it was that Charles went to a mid-week prayer service at Hope of the World Pentecostal Church. Frankie made clear that her whole family would be going, so Charles asked if he should ride with them. "No," she said, "you and I'll go in your car, because you might decide to leave early."

The church was a drab, wooden structure that Charles had undoubtedly passed but never truly seen: basically one big room, filled with folding metal chairs facing a piano, a music stand, and a large wooden cross. The only other item that served as decoration was an obviously homemade, felt banner that read, "I am the resurrection and the life," with a felt lily pasted in the corner.

Clyde and family were already there when Charles and Frankie arrived. Her mother had saved two seats on the end of their row, but Frankie whispered to her, and then steered Charles to the middle of a row across the center aisle. "I don't think you'll want to be on the end," she told him.

As they sat listening to the friendly chatter around them, Charles found himself wondering who all these people were. If they lived in Savannah County, he'd never seen them. Well, he did sort of know the Robinsons who lived on Stringville Road; and there was Roxanne-what's-her-name who was in his class or a year ahead, although she looked different in this setting; and he had seen that man near the front selling tomatoes at the market on the square; and, come to think of it, he did know Mrs. Copeland who lived near his grandparent's old house. He counted the number of Black people in the room: twelve, thirteen, fourteen. As far as he knew, there was only one Black family in Lockwood, so these people must come from Lincoln

County where there was more industry. Or maybe, the thought came to him, they were farmers. Could that be?

The service didn't seem to have an official beginning, at least not like what he was used to. It just started when a man in a white, short-sleeved shirt, who Charles guessed was Reverend Miller, shouted, "Worship the Lord with gladness! Come into his presence with singing! Those who know the Lord are glad!" And, suddenly, the pianist was playing and they were all singing, "He has made me glad, he has made me glad. I will rejoice, for he has made me glad!" But it was how they sang, nearly everyone clapping or with hands in the air, the minister pacing back and forth, occasionally shouting, "Praise the Lord! Praise him! Let me hear you praise him. Show him you are *glad*!" And it seemed to Charles that the people around him were glad. He found himself clapping, with increasing vigor, along with Frankie, who from time to time glanced at him and smiled

And then, without break, they were singing, "Holy, holy God almighty. I will lift you up and magnify your name," the minister now joined in front by an older woman, a kerchief on her head, who led the singing. It was unlike anything Charles had ever experienced, certainly in church: several people jumping in place; a woman in a wheelchair (yes, he also had seen her before) rocking back and forth; two people, including Clyde's son Scott, dancing wildly in front, while two others, who looked almost in a trance, were lowered to their knees by the pastor. He now understood why Frankie had them move, because people on

163

the end of their row were out in the aisle. And yet, he thought, there was also something . . . normal about it all. In front of him, a woman who had been violently shaking stopped to twist her hair into a coil and pin it on the crown of her head. Another woman sat playing with an infant, as if nothing special were happening around her. And, when he looked across the aisle, Charles saw that Clyde was seated, head bowed, his wife's arm around his shoulders.

At some point, the singing gave way to praying. "Be healed," said the minister. "Feel the Spirit's power in your bones, in your muscles, in your joints, in your mind, in your heart, in your soul." Charles found that he was thinking of—yes, praying for—Clyde.

And then the minister was preaching, but in an informal way, punctuated by frequent *Amens* and *Praise the Lords* from the congregation. His text, which Frankie followed in a Bible she apparently carried in her oversized purse, was from Psalm 51: "Have mercy upon me, O God, according to thy loving kindness . . . . Wash me thoroughly from mine iniquity, and cleanse me from my sin. For I acknowledge my transgressions: and my sin is ever before me."

"Brothers and sisters," said the minister, "this is the truth about us: we are sinners, shot through with iniquity." Again, lots of *Amens*. "As the Apostle says, the good things we want to do, we don't do 'em. Not most of the time, anyway. There is evil in every heart." *Amen!* "But, hallelujah! There's also good in us because God made us, and there is mercy in the Lord, if we'll just ask him for it. If we know the bad news, we can praise God with true gladness for the good."

When the *Praise the Lords* died away, the minister was silent, walking back and forth, not looking at the congregation. "Some of you," he said at last, "have asked me, 'Brother Lionel, what about these riots in Detroit? That's no way for people to act,' you've said to me. You've said, 'These rioters are sinful.'" Charles glanced at Frankie, but her attention was completely on the preacher. "I understand what you're sayin', but, friends, let's remember what Paul says in Romans, three and twenty-three: All have sinned and fallen short." Scattered *Amens*. "Not just the rioters, but those whose greed and uppity ways makes other folks feel like they have to riot just to be seen." More *Amens*. "So, brothers and sisters, let's not forget the sin behind the sin when we're talkin' about who's a sinner." Charles found that he was leaning forward in the metal chair, and that Frankie had taken his hand.

Chapter Eight

Charles hated it when people called him skinny. His mother had often assured him that he would fill out *someday*, although her language was hardly comforting: "After all, your great aunt is fat and your father is getting paunchy." And *someday* had certainly not happened during high school.

So it was with amazement that he realized he had gained nine and a quarter pounds this summer. It began with breakfast. For years, his standard fare was a bowl of Frosted Flakes, often gulped down on his way out the door. Now, however, even though he had to be at the garage by 7:30, Charles got up in time to fix two or three pieces of toast, with jelly, to go with his cereal; and sometimes he also scrambled two or three eggs, with cheese—and ate a banana. It also didn't hurt that, whenever he could talk Jerry into it, they would take their break at the 7-Eleven, where he would have a large Slurpee (and watch hopefully for Frankie), not to mention that he was drinking a lot of beer.

The truly amazing thing, however, was the way these extra calories transmogrified into actual muscle. Some days, after lifting sacks of cement or shoveling piles of dirt, his shoulders and arms were so tired he could hardly move (except around Frankie). But it was a good tired, because he could practically feel his muscles getting bigger and more defined, at least compared to the start of the summer. He could also see the difference when he flexed in front of the hall mirror, although he was careful to do this when Connie wasn't around.

Occasionally, he even wore T-shirts when he didn't have to, including when he picked up Frankie on Saturday afternoon, the third week of August. That morning there had been more trash around the square than usual, and Charles had been worried he and Moss would be late getting back to the garage. But Moss goosed the old truck until it was going nearly fifty, and they rolled in a little before noon. On the way to the dump, Charles had recounted his experience at Wednesday's Pentecostal service, and even though he never mentioned Frankie, Moss seemed to get the picture. "Love," he said, "makes us do crazy things. I don't think that's from Shakespeare, but it could've been."

Charles thought he and Frankie might see a movie, drive his still-new-to-him car up to Mahaska. But Frankie pointed out that, unlike him, she had been inside all week. What if they went for a hike? When Charles said "Sure, that sounds like fun," he immediately pictured the well-marked trails around Lake

168

Winyan. Frankie, however, had in mind a hilly, wooded corner of a farm owned by one of Clyde's friends, almost on the Missouri border; and after an hour of difficult terrain, Charles, unlike Frankie, was exhausted. So much for being in shape.

"I have a great aunt and uncle who live near here," he told Frankie, while plopping down on a stump. "What if we head over there and have a glass of iced tea?" She turned to face him, and he was suddenly struck by how . . . enchanting she looked with shafts of light falling on her through the trees, her brown, shoulder-length hair blowing gently. So what if she was in an over-sized T-shirt and baggy sweatpants. What a contrast to Nancy who had complained about bugs and humidity whenever they had done anything outdoors, except play golf, which she did in color-coordinated outfits. Maybe, he thought, this is more—

She interrupted his reverie. "You haven't seemed very eager to introduce me to your family. Are you sure you want to do this?" The corners of her mouth twitched with the hint of a smile.

"Why would I have to introduce you? I mean, my mom and dad already know you." When she raised her eyebrows, he added, "Well, they know who you are and see you around town; you said my dad used to say hello to you; so anyway, Auntie, my dad's aunt, is *very* different from my dad. It's like they're not even related."

By the time they got there, around 4:00, his great uncle Claude had closed the store and gone fishing at a favorite pond.

169

Auntie was resting, but clearly delighted by their visit. "Come in! Come in! You two look like you've been doing something outside in this heat."

Charles started to introduce Frankie, but Auntie was well ahead of him. "You are the lovely young lady who is always so friendly and helpful at that store in Lockwood."

"Fashion on the Square."

"Yes, yes, Fashion on the Square. One time I was in there, and a woman—I won't say who, but she was a friend of Charles' grandmother—was complaining that the companies had changed their sizes, and you were so patient with her," a remark that made Charles and Frankie smile. "Sit, sit. I'll get some iced tea. You must be thirsty. They call you Frankie, don't they? Do you take sugar, Frankie?" Frankie started to say "No, thank you," but Auntie continued, "Well, I'll get it just in case. And Claude just picked the last of the blackberries, so you'll have to have a piece of blackberry pie. We will never eat it all. Charles always looks like he needs a piece of whatever I've got around here." Then realizing her *faux pas*, she added, "Well, *both* of you look . . . well, not skinny. Charles doesn't like people saying he's skinny, but . . . like you could use some pie."

Frankie took her off the hook by changing the subject. "Did you crochet all of these doilies?"

"Why, yes, except for the ones from my mother, Charles' great grandmother, who lived right here in Savannah County. He has deep roots here."

170

"They're beautiful, so intricate."

"Why thank you, dear. I don't think Charles likes things like that very much, do you Charles?" Before Charles could answer, one way or the other, Auntie asked him, "How are things on the street crew? I admire how they keep the town looking so nice. And how they keep the dust down in the summer, which just gets all over everything, if you let it."

"Actually," said Charles, "Jerry and I are doing a survey of the gravel streets, so Clyde will know which ones need oil and sand on them."

"Isn't that just like you, Charles, always using your head! Now, you two just stay there while I fix things," but Frankie followed her into the kitchen, and Charles could hear them talking, and even laughing, while he sat facing the old family pictures on the wall above the chairs where Auntie and Claude sat every evening.

When they returned with tea, and pie with ice cream, Auntie was saying, ". . . so since we didn't have children of our own, Charles and Connie have been extra special to us." Charles had skipped lunch (except for an apple and a leftover sandwich and some chips and a small, stale cookie) in his haste to pick up Frankie, so he was ready for blackberry pie and ice cream, but the two women were now looking at the framed photographs, including one of his mother that Frankie homed in on immediately.

"How beautiful she is."

171

"Yes, and I've always thought Charles looks like his mother. Of course, he has his father's ears, which he's grown into, but he has her brown eyes and nice cheekbones."

Frankie looked back quickly, smiling. "His cheekbones are one of my favorite parts."

"I think Madeleine told me she was twenty when that was taken," said Auntie. "About what you are now. She hadn't yet met Robert, and I think she was just getting ready to start teaching, which, you know, she stopped when Connie was born. I don't think Robert liked her working so much. I'm not sure why, but she wanted me to have this for my picture wall."

Charles wanted to ask more about his mother's teaching, but Frankie was saying, "Look at those clothes! Look how the jacket's collar and pockets match that perfectly-fitted skirt," which was hard for Charles to discern since the photograph was black and white. "Was that taken in Des Moines? I bet no one in Lockwood was dressed as fancy as this."

Charles looked more closely at the picture of his mother, but the two women were now examining a photo of Charles receiving a prize for something or other, and one of him in his Little League uniform.

"I wasn't much of a ballplayer," he said peering over their shoulders and touching Frankie gently.

"I don't know anything about that," said Auntie, "but I know people talked about how they made you a coach when you were just a boy, probably because you're so smart."

172

Charles could feel his ears turning red. "Our manager didn't have any adult who wanted to do it, so since I wasn't in the game, he told me to be the third-base coach. That's all."

"But I remember your father talking about it."

"Yeah, well, that's because I waved a baserunner home, in a big game down in Keosauqua, and he got thrown out by a mile. That's why he was talking about it. For days and days and days he was talking about it."

He suddenly realized that Frankie was watching him, with an expression almost . . . tender. She turned to Auntie. "You know, Charles could just stick to things he's good at, like books, but he doesn't." She smiled. "It's one of the things I . . . like about him. My father says Charles didn't know which end of the hammer to use when he started working with the street crew, but he kept at it."

"Your father is the nicest man," said Auntie, as she ushered them and the melting ice cream to the dining room table, a comment that again made Charles and Frankie smile and glance at each other.

"He has his good days," said Frankie.

"Eat, eat," said Auntie. Before they could take a bite, however, she added, "You'll have to forgive all the questions, but Charles has never brought a girlfriend here before." Charles pressed his leg against Frankie's under the heavy, oak table. "Did you know each other from school? Are you both going to Drake? How long have you been dating?"

173

There was what felt to Charles like an awkward pause before he said, "Not long. Really, just a few weeks."

"Well," said Auntie, "you just seem so natural together. You must have a lot in common."

Another awkward pause before Frankie asked, "How did you and your husband meet?"

"Oh, heavens! I haven't thought about that in a coon's age. Back in our day, young people didn't have so many choices. If Claude and I'd grown up today, I don't know if we'd ever have got together." She closed her eyes and rocked slightly from side to side. "He was so shy, and he didn't even graduate from high school. But was there ever a nicer man? It all just worked out."

"You were blessed."

"You are so right, Frankie! That's the word for it. That must be another thing you two have in common."

"What's that?" asked Charles.

"Why, going to church. You have always been such a regular churchgoer, Charles. Is that where you first got to know each other?"

"Actually," he told her, with a mouthful of pie, "we go to different churches."

"Oh, they can't be that different, unless it's a Negro church like those ones over in Lincoln County. But you wouldn't go to one of *those*," she said looking at Frankie.

Charles and Frankie finished their pie without speaking, eyes on their plates while Auntie talked about Claude and his fishing, and how Charles used to go with him from time to time, although he clearly didn't love it the way Claude does. Then, for some reason, she talked about how Charles called the rolling terrain between there and the Missouri border the tickly hills, and how they used to make him car sick when he sat in the back seat. When she seemed ready to recount an episode of sickness, Charles started to interrupt, but in fact, she was on to a new topic: the puzzle maps she used to keep in the closet for Charles, because he did love those, a lot more than fishing. When he was knee high to a grasshopper, she got him a puzzle of the United States, and as he got older, a puzzle of all the world's countries. "There wasn't a one he didn't know," she marveled. "Could put that puzzle together in no time. He probably got that from his mother who is always thinking about other places."

Frankie finished her tea and said, "Thank you, Aunt Vera."

"Oh Frankie, I wish you would call me Auntie. That's what Charles has always called me . . . and Connie, too."

"Thank you . . . Auntie. I should have told you a minute ago, when we were talking about it, that Charles has come to my church, just last week. And I think he enjoyed it." Charles started to add his agreement, but Frankie spoke over him. "We're a real mix of folks in my church, including some from Lincoln County. As Clyde always says, God cares a lot more about the engine and the transmission than the coat of paint." But by then, Auntie was busy pouring more tea and may not have heard all that Frankie was saying.

175

They left before Claude got home, despite Auntie's protests. "Well, come back when you can stay longer," she told them. Frankie did pause for a minute to sit on the porch swing, saying how much she wished her family had one of these; and while she was gently swinging, Auntie whispered to Charles, "Bring her back for a meal. As Claude would say, she's a keeper."

Neither of them spoke as Charles pulled away from Eaton's Grocery and General Store and headed north toward Lockwood. After they had gone little more than a half mile, Frankie said, "I do like her, you know," and then, before Charles could answer, she added, "Turn right. Here," gesturing with her hand. "I want to show you a special place, special for me . . . and Clyde."

"Does some relative of yours live out here?"

"No, it's just a place. I'll show you."

He turned the Buick onto the barely-graveled, deeply-rutted road, driving slowly past cornfields with stunted stalks along the edges, past fields of alfalfa, across a one-lane bridge, with no cars visible in either direction. Since the land here was flat, they could see a cluster of trees in the distance, indicating the presence of a farmhouse. Frankie told him to stop.

She turned in the seat to face him. "Remember in the restaurant when I told you I had been in an accident with a tractor?" Charles nodded, but Frankie was now looking out the window at the side of the road. "This is where it was. Clyde came out here to help a friend pick up his bales of hay, and my brothers came along to help, so, of course, I tagged along. I think

I was eight. Seven or eight. Anyway, this friend was too poor to own a wagon—Clyde told me this later—so he borrowed a sled, logs sawed in half and bound together, that they dragged behind the tractor."

"I've never even seen one of those."

"Well, they had one, take my word for it, and it was so heavy it took four men to lift a corner of it. They were taking it back to the farmer who owned it, in this house right up here. I had just been sitting around in the shade while Larry and Scott were working, and I wanted to be part of it—that's what Clyde says—so he said that when we returned the sled I could ride on the tractor. It was an old one with a toolbox behind the seat, and he told me to stand on that." Frankie closed her eyes as she continued talking. "I have this memory of riding up there, holding on to the seat, waving to Clyde and my brothers in the pickup behind us." She waved her hand as if recreating the scene. "But then I guess Clyde's friend turned around to make sure I was holding on or something, and when he did the front wheels of the tractor hit a giant pothole."

Frankie stopped, apparently reliving the scene in her mind, until Charles asked, "What happened?"

"Next thing I remember is being under the sled with the dust in my nose and mouth. Right here." She pointed to the side of the road. "And then there was my daddy, lifting the sled and holding it up with one arm while he yanked me out with the other."

They sat silently for a minute before Charles said, "I don't think you've told many people about this, have you?"

Frankie smiled. "Look how shallow the ditch is alongside the road. Hardly a ditch at all. But it was just deep enough that I fell in it and the sled didn't crush me when it whipsawed behind the tractor. It took the skin right off my shoulder, but missed my head." She pulled the neck of the over-sized T-shirt until her shoulder was bare. "All that's left is this scar."

Charles leaned over to see more closely, and then gently ran his finger along the pale ridge of scar tissue. He thought of leaning to kiss it, but Frankie straightened her T-shirt and sat upright. "No," she said softly, "I haven't told others. I think of this as a kind of holy place." Frankie seemed to have more to say, and Charles, perhaps becoming less a novice at adulthood, waited. "I think I must have been saved for a reason."

Charles could feel his heart beating faster. "What do you think it is?"

Frankie looked at him and smiled. "Do you remember Mrs. Sylvester who taught English? I remember one time she asked me, 'What are you passionate about?' That, she said, will be a sign of what you're called to do, and the worst thing is to be trapped doing something all your life that isn't your passion. I think she meant being in the wrong job, but I also think she was talking about being in the wrong place . . . or with the wrong person." She cleared her throat. "I didn't ask her, but I wanted to, 'What if you don't have a choice? What if the hand God deals you is working in dead-end jobs in a dying town? What if your passion is something that's not possible in your circumstances?'" She cleared her throat again, and smiled. "But since then I've been thinking that if you're saved for a reason, none of that matters. You just have to discover the reason God has in mind for you wherever you are and whatever you're doing."

She looked at Charles' face and laughed out loud. "I know, that all sounds pretty weird, but it's what I think about when I don't intend to think about anything. Your turn. Tell me something weird you think about."

Charles sat for a minute, Frankie's eyes on his profile. "One of the daydreams I keep having while I'm working is coming back to Lockwood, I guess after making lots of money, and telling Dexter I had a house built for him, with a big porch, on that lake somewhere in the Ozarks." He could feel his ears turning red. "You know. Superhero! Rides in to save the day," trying to make it all sound jocular.

Frankie slid closer and kissed him on the cheek. "That's not weird, it's sweet." She kept her head on his shoulder for ten seconds, twenty seconds, before saying, "Let's go." And then in a voice so soft Charles could hardly hear it, "Maybe someday I'll let you see my real scars."

Charles had hoped, even expected, they would spend the evening together, maybe drive to Mahaska and have dinner or see a movie; but as they approached Lockwood, the courthouse and water tower coming into view, Frankie told him she was needed at home.

"Does it have to do with Clyde?"

"Why would you ask that?"

"I know, everybody knows, that he hasn't been feeling well, so—"

"Charles, I don't have to give you a reason for everything I do, do I? You still have your life with lots of things I don't know about, and I have mine."

He got home around 6:30, and, since there didn't seem to be any dinner, rummaged in the refrigerator to find the fixings for a sandwich—or two. He was putting what he found on the counter when his mother entered the kitchen.

"I assumed you were going to be out," she told him. "I didn't fix any dinner because Connie's spending the night at Julie's, and your father is doing a golf scramble, whatever that is. I think they just play until it's too dark to see the ball, and then sit in the clubhouse and drink—and tell stories."

"About growing up in Savannah County."

His mother smiled. "Yes, stories about Savannah County. It's hard to imagine being *chauviniste* about a corner of a state, but to each his own, I guess."

Charles had been putting mustard on his ham and turkey and roast beef with cheese sandwich, but he now turned to face his mother. "Women do things like that at the Country Club. Why don't you ever do that?"

"Can you imagine me at a golf scramble?! The Country Club is really your dad's thing. *Je vais juste s'il y a de la nourriture*—and fireworks."

"You remember right after I found the body when Dad and I had a talk in his study?" His mother nodded. "He told me that living in Lockwood was all his idea, that you wanted to stay in Des Moines."

His mother busied herself straightening a dish towel by the sink. "Oh, things happen," she said, after a pause. "You marry someone and you always end up doing some things you wouldn't have done otherwise."

Charles took his sandwich and pile of chips to the kitchen table. After he was seated and had taken a few bites, she said, "I got a call a few minutes ago from Auntie." Charles glanced at her before taking another bite. "She told me you went there with Frankie." This was the first time he had heard his mother say the name.

"Yeah, we were in that part of the county, so dropped in to have some iced tea."

"Well, your great aunt couldn't stop talking about how 'natural'—that's the word she kept using, 'natural'—you seemed together." Charles continued to eat, eyes on his plate. "I told her you were just going out with her for the summer. A few weeks, really. That's right, isn't it? It's not a serious relationship . . ." When Charles looked up, she was staring at him. He shrugged.

"Charles!" her voice now louder. "You are about to begin a new chapter of your life, get out of Lockwood. The last thing you want is to be tied down here."

"How do you know what I want?"

"All right . . . the last thing you *need*. This is a time in your life to try new things, explore who you are. Maybe spend a year abroad. Drake has those programs, you know, including to France. And we have the money for you to have experiences most people only dream of."

"People like Frankie." Before she could respond, he added, "If you want me to explore who I am, then let me do it my way, not just the way you would choose. I'm not you—or Dad." He slid his chair back, picked up his plate, and headed back to the counter. "I bet you would like Frankie, if you got to know her."

"If you wanted us to know her," said his mother, "you could have brought her by the house. We've always been welcoming to your friends."

"So Connie can spend the whole time talking about how great Nancy is? No thanks."

His mother sighed and refolded the towel. "Connie says that Frankie—"

"Who cares what Connie says! Frankie is a good person. Jerry knows her from high school, and he thinks she's great. She's fun. She cares about people. I had three classes with her, and she's . . . a good student. More than that, she knows how to listen so that she can practically read your mind." His words, he

182

realized, were sounding less ambivalent than he sometimes felt. But they *were* true, weren't they?

When his mother next spoke, her tone had softened. "I am sure, *mon fils, mon magnifique fils,* that Frankie is a very nice young woman. But does she have . . . plans? Is she saving money to go to college? Surely she isn't going to work at Fashion on the Square all her life."

Charles put away the last of the sandwich stuff. "Not everybody," he said as he left the kitchen, "is as blessed as I am."

The following week the fair came to Savannah County. When Charles was a kid, the county fair was always a highlight of the summer. He liked the food—corn dogs, ice cream sandwiches, tenderloins that stuck out way beyond the bun—and, especially, sitting in his family's box in the grandstand, right on the finish line, to watch the stock car races. He and Nancy had sat together in the box for practically every race and evening concert the last two years, sometimes dressing up as if they were at Churchill Downs. This year, however, the fair's arrival seemed to sneak up on him, even though multi-colored posters advertising "Savannah County Fair, August 23-27, at the Fairgrounds in Lockwood" were stapled all over town, including on the public notice board outside the city office.

Now that Charles had gone to church with Frankie's family, he stopped picking her up near the courthouse. Besides, as

Connie had pointed out more than once, everyone knew they were dating. So, on Thursday the 24th, he cleaned up quickly after work and then drove straight to her family's porchless house, with its peeling yellow paint, an old pickup rusting out back. Frankie had said she would meet him in front, but he was early and unsure of what to do. Knock on the front door, even though it would mean the dogs would go crazy in the backyard, or just wait? He decided on the former; but when Frankie opened the door, Charles had a clear view of Clyde, salt and pepper crewcut where his baseball cap usually sat, bent double in an old, overstuffed chair. Frankie started to close the door part way, but realizing it was too late, simply turned and said, "Bye, Daddy." Clyde raised his hand, but didn't look up. "Is there anything—?"

"Just go," he said.

It was a short drive to the fairgrounds, and Frankie filled it with talk that avoided the obvious subject. She told Charles how she, too, had always looked forward to the county fair, although her memories of it made him think they had attended different fairs. One time, she told him, she had actually seen the caravan of midway attractions snaking its way down Highway 52 and into the fairgrounds, and she had felt a thrill wondering what it would be like to travel that way from town to town, setting up, watching people, tearing down, moving on. As he parked the Buick in the big, grassy lot, Charles raised the possibility of joining his family in their box for the evening's program, but it was something of a relief to both of them when she said no.

184

Instead, they headed for the midway, where Charles insisted they ride the Tilt-a-Whirl so he could enjoy the feeling of Frankie's body smashed against his. Then, since she also seemed to enjoy this, they rode the flying swings for the same reason, although it appeared to Charles that the operator was leering at his girlfriend. That's what she was, wasn't she? That's what Auntie had called her: his *girlfriend.*

Charles, at Frankie's urging, tried his luck at knocking over weighted milk bottles, watched while she shot at pop-up ducks, and, after being egged on by the barker, even tried to ring a bell at the top of a tall column by striking a lever with a wooden mallet, something he wouldn't have dreamed of doing three months earlier. The first two times he came up short, though not by much; but on the third try, the bell mercifully rang, and onlookers applauded. His prize was a small, stuffed bear, which he, of course, gave to Frankie, who promptly gave it to a young girl standing nearby with her mother. "I know them from church," she told him, although the woman's reaction told Charles that might not be true.

They stopped for ice cream in a waffle cone, Frankie insisting they split it, and gently wiping his shirt when it turned out the cone leaked. They also split a corn dog after the smell proved too appealing. While eating it, they exchanged greetings with a high school teacher and a friend of Charles' family, neither of whom asked him about finding the body. That, he realized, was no longer news. They talked for a while with

185

friends of hers, then with friends who knew them both; but when he saw Randall, Cliff, and Kenny at a nearby booth, Charles wasn't sure whether he wanted to meet them or go the other direction. Surely, it wasn't that he was embarrassed to be seen with Frankie. All his friends ever did was talk about girls, while he, at least, was with one—one they would like a lot, he told himself, if they got to know her. (Although he did wish she had worn one of the blouses she sold at Fashion on the Square instead of this western-looking shirt with squiggly stuff above the pockets that ended in arrow points.) He didn't really think they would smirk or act stupid, at least until he and Frankie were out of sight. And he wanted to ask Randall if the story about him being followed home by the sheriff was true. But for some reason, these friends of his past didn't quite fit with his present.

He suggested to Frankie they go the other way, past a juggler and a sword swallower in medieval costume. And then they were at the display barns, an area of the fairgrounds where Charles-of-the-grandstand-box had never set foot.

"Let's go in."

"I've spent enough time in those barns," said Frankie. "Mom and I used to enter pies in the competition, and I had to stand there, sometimes it seemed like all day, while the judges tasted all of them."

"You made pies for a competition at the fair? What kind?"

"All kinds. But our best one," she told him, heading the other direction, "was rhubarb."

He took her arm and gently pulled her toward the large, sliding door, beyond which were bright lights and the smell of hay. "You can show me where you used to hang out."

Once inside, Frankie looked around and seemed to relax. They had been holding hands, but now she let go. "I'll tell you something about me you don't know. When I was little, Clyde had a few horses, two or three at a time that he kept out at Grandpa Simmons' farm. Whoever bought the farm let him use the barn, and we took care of those horses and went riding out there . . . especially, I remember, on a path by a stream. It was so pretty: water flowing over the rocks, wildflowers . . . ." She smiled. "He told me one of the ponies was mine. I called her Rhubarb, because she was kind of reddish, and she won a ribbon right here in this barn. My picture was in the paper, although not on the front page." She looked up at him and smiled again.

"What happened to the pony?" asked Charles. "Clyde doesn't still have horses, does he?"

"Clyde loves horses. He grew up around horses, but I guess you knew that." Her voice got softer, and he had to strain to hear her above the hum of surrounding conversations. "It just got too expensive to keep them. I remember when he finally had to sell mine. I was ten, and he told me not to cry. Told me sad things would happen all my life, and I might as well get used to it."

"That's pretty harsh!"

"Was he wrong?"

They wandered for a minute past rows of canned vegetables and fruit, past cages of chickens, past a beautiful display of a wide variety of roses. He took her hand again, or maybe it was she who took his, as they stopped in front of a board advertising the antique tractor show, chicken bingo, and Saturday's crowning of the Savannah County Fair queen, with pictures of the three finalists and a promise of prizes from, among others, Fashion on the Square.

"Have you ever been, you know, nominated for queen?"

She turned to look at him and laughed. "I think something has messed up your judgment, sweetheart."

The word caught him up short, and it was a few seconds before he could stammer, "Why would you say that? You are smart, and you are . . . beautiful."

"Charles, please, I am not beautiful." She paused. "But sometimes, when I'm with you, I feel . . . pretty."

He wanted to kiss her right there, but she had moved on. He followed her around a corner, past the table where pies would later be displayed, back into the main part of the barn, where a young man in cowboy boots and a baseball cap with John Deere written across it, someone he distantly knew from high school, appeared before them.

"If it isn't Frankie. I didn't know if I'd see you in a place like this anymore." He smiled, at least with his lips. "But I see you haven't forgot your old friends altogether."

"Hello, Irvin." She took Charles' arm and began to pull him toward the sliding door.

"Oh, come on, Frankie. I saw you come in, so I know you just got here." His eyes never left her as he said, "Why don't you show Mister Top-of-the-Class here what animals look like."

Frankie wheeled to face him, bumping Charles behind her with her hip as she did so. "Irvin, don't make a scene and embarrass yourself. Just go back to whatever you were doing."

The smile was gone. "So now you're too good for farmers like me, is that it? You seemed to like me just fine 'bout this time last year," reaching as he said this for Frankie's arm.

And then things happened quickly. Charles later remembered stepping from behind Frankie and telling Irvin to back off, or something such, before Irvin pushed him hard in the chest and he stumbled backwards over an unfortunately placed bale of hay. Which is why he missed the moment when Scott, coming up from behind, put Irvin in a chokehold. The farmer was turning red as Charles got to his feet, Frankie yelling for her brother to let him breathe, a crowd now gathering. When the dust and straw settled, Irvin was on the floor of the barn, and Charles heard Scott say, "I don't give a shit about him, but don't ever put your hands on my sister again."

They left the fairgrounds soon after. When Charles asked Frankie if she wanted to go again on Friday, she said Clyde needed her to do some things for him, and they left it at that.

Chapter Nine

The plan from the beginning of the summer was that Charles' last day of work with the street crew would be Friday, September 1, since he had to leave for Drake immediately after Labor Day. As that day drew closer, Charles told Clyde he would be happy to help Moss with the garbage run on Saturday the 2nd—sort of take his street crew duties full circle—but Clyde said no. It was time to start turning his attention from things in Lockwood toward things in Des Moines, a comment that Charles wasn't sure how to interpret.

Jerry's last day, however, was a week earlier, because he needed to leave for Iowa City on Tuesday the 29th. I've got things to take care of, he had told Charles. Maybe a few things to smooth over. And so Charles came up with the idea of inviting the street crew and their wives to his home—his father's home— on Monday the 28th for a cookout. It would be a way of saying goodbye to Jerry and celebrating, or at least acknowledging, the work they had all done together.

191

It was his mother who talked him out of it. "I realize that this summer has been important for you, but it's not the same for them," she told him. "You've given them a hand for three months; these men are there for years. You've just made a guest appearance in their lives."

"You don't understand!" his voice a real contrast to her calm, rational tone. "They are my friends."

"Charles, they wouldn't feel comfortable coming to a cookout at this house."

"How do you know? I'm the one who works with them every day."

"Trust me on this. Some things you just learn by living a few years."

And so Charles, with Jerry's half-hearted support, decided to invite the street crew and their wives to a cookout in the city park. "Come right after work, at least by 5:30," he said to them while gathered around the couch and workbench. "I'll start a fire for some hot dogs, and Jerry's bringing beer. You don't need to bring a thing."

They did come—Clyde, Dexter, and Moss—but not their wives, each of them indicating he had to get home soon. And the beer clearly made them nervous. "If Woody comes by," said Clyde, looking over his shoulder, "he won't trouble you boys much. It's our asses he'll kick."

They were gone by 6:15, leaving Charles and Jerry to clean up the scant evidence of the cookout, and then to say goodbye to each other. Charles started to say how he was grateful Jerry had been so friendly to him, but that sounded too . . . something, so he stopped. Jerry started to tell Charles to loosen up and have fun in college, but he, too, halted in mid-sentence. They settled for promises to have a beer when they both were back in town. *"Au revoir et bonne chance á vous,"* said Jerry. Charles started to say, "I hope you mean *á toi,*" but instead gave a short wave. And that was it.

It was raining lightly, and the sky was heavy with moisture, as Charles got to work on Tuesday. Clyde wasn't there at 7:30, so Dexter, Moss, and Charles sat or leaned in their usual places, no one mentioning the cookout, until Clyde arrived just before 8:00 in a foul mood. "Can't none of you think of somethin' needs doin' if I ain't here to think of it for you?" The sound of Moss cracking his knuckles made Clyde turn in his direction. "Doin' nothin'. If I ain't here, all of you start actin' like Moss."

Charles felt he should say something, point out that it was raining, point out that it was barely 8:00, point out that Clyde himself often sat there in the morning before announcing the day's work; but, to his amazement, it was Moss who spoke, not directly to Clyde, but looking past all of them at the back wall. "My name is Jim. That's my name: Jim. When I taught school, nobody knew my name either." He paused. "But at least there I was Mr. Moss."

It was Charles who broke the prolonged silence that followed. "Maybe, Clyde, I should go up to Harry's and pick up those tubing wrenches the city ordered."

Clyde stared at his pipe for a minute, and then without looking up said, "Yeah, you do that."

"Maybe Moss—Jim—should come with me."

"Just go. I still decide who does what."

But Harry's, as Charles should have known, doesn't open until 8:30 on weekdays. Now what to do? He was wandering in the light rain, back toward the garage, when he saw his father, and his father's usual circle of coffee buddies, waving to him from the long table visible in the front window of the West Side Café. It was Harry, himself, who pulled a chair from a neighboring table and signaled Ginny to bring another mug. "Have a seat. The street crew can't be doing much work in this weather."

"Unless," said Mr. Firmin, the insurance agent, "Clyde ever gets around to cleaning out that storm sewer in front of the bank."

The men all chuckled, and two of them began to talk at once: "Remember that time it rained hard and the water was up on the sidewalk." "I can still see old Clarence out there in his ten-piece suit pulling up wet leaves and whatever." More chuckling, while Charles fiddled with the tall, fluted sugar dispenser.

"You have had quite a summer," said Mr. Firmin, once the others stopped talking, "what with the storm and then finding

194

that body at Mars Hill. You're probably ready to get back to the books." Charles smiled and nodded politely, but the conversation was already off on a different track.

"I hear they now say he was from Missoura. Nick something."

"I thought Woody said his mother came here from Arkansas to identify the body."

"That's what he told me, too."

"I need to get up there and see what's left of the church," this from his father.

"If it wasn't so durn far out in the country. I went there once and like to never found my way."

It was the local judge who brought the conversation back to Charles. "Are you excited? I imagine you've been spending a lot of time getting ready, your first time living away from home. In fact, I'm a bit surprised you are still working. Your dad told us you leave right after Labor Day."

"Actually," said Charles, "I haven't thought about it much at all." That sounded rude, so he added, "But I'm sure I'll begin to feel it this week."

"That was the problem for my Ronnie." This from Frank who ran Western Auto. "You said it, Judge. Getting ready is important, and he never got himself ready." He looked around the table, and the other men nodded sympathetically. "There wasn't any reason for him to come back here and go to community college over in Centerville. No girlfriend, nothing like that. He's not as smart as Charles, but he's no dummy. He just wasn't ready to be in a place with ten times more students than Lockwood has people."

"Who'd want to be on some of them campuses nowadays," said a sixty-ish, heavy-set man everyone called Junior. "You see what they're doing now, burning draft cards and what not? Right up here in Wisconsin."

This time it was Charles' father who pulled the conversation back. "You would have to say, Frank, that Ron's now got a good job and a nice family. There are different ways to grow up, and it just takes some a little longer."

Others nodded, and Frank said, "Yeah, he's doing all right. But I feel like he missed something important by not sticking it out up at Ames, at least for a year or two."

While Frank took a sip of coffee, the judge said, "That's why I asked Charles about getting ready. But then, I'm sure," he looked around the table, "that Charles has things under control."

Charles listened, mostly staring at the rings made by his coffee mug on the paper placemat, as they discussed whether this rain was too late to help the corn and soybeans—as if, he said to himself, any of them actually did any farming. He listened as they discussed what to do with the vacant stores on the square, as if they were going to do anything more than talk about it. "Young people just don't want to stay in a town like this," said Mr. Firmin the insurance agent, "or move here from somewhere else," added Harry the hardware store owner.

196

"The problem," said Charles, perhaps too softly, "is that people in Savannah County don't like the ones who might want to move here, like the—" but two men had already jumped into the conversation and the others appeared not to have heard him. And so he just listened as they discussed the sheriff's now-closed investigation into the death at Mars Hill, and how they were sure there was more to the story than Woody was letting on, as if he, Charles, sitting right there beside them, wasn't the one person in town with first-hand information!

"Thanks for the coffee," he said when there was a break in the flow of words. Then, forgetting why he had come to the square, added, "I need to get back to the garage."

"What for?" asked Junior. "I bet you can't be getting much done, especially with Clyde being sick. Those boys are just sitting on that old sofa—have you seen the dirt in that thing?— shootin' the breeze, trying to avoid as much work as they can." He turned to the others, with a big smile on his face. "I hear Woody picked up Moss earlier this summer doing twenty on the highway so he wouldn't have to get back to work." Charles was at least glad his father didn't laugh.

"He was going at least forty. I was with him. If you want to know what really happened, I can give you the real story. And he couldn't go much faster or that truck would fall apart." This was not said softly. When no one immediately spoke, Charles continued, "Maybe you all need to come up with more money so the city can buy a decent truck."

197

"Yeah, Robert," said Harry, grinning. "You hear your son? You're on the city council. Quit spending money on a fancy ball diamond and buy these fellas a new truck."

This time they all laughed, before Junior, his big smile in place, added, "So Moss can strip its gears and Clyde can ruin the transmission pullin' out that tractor whenever he gets it stuck somewhere." Charles pushed his chair back abruptly, the legs scraping on the old linoleum floor, and started to stand up but Junior, at least, didn't seem to notice. "The one that tickles me is Dexter, with his big plans. One day I said to him, 'Dexter, you don't still have that crazy idea of retirin' on the Lake of the Ozarks, do you?'" A couple of the men chuckled, and Charles could feel his ears turn red.

He was now on his feet. "Why would you say such a thing?!" His vehemence was obviously a surprise to all except his father who sat staring at his coffee mug, lips pursed. "What good did it do to ask him that?"

Now Junior wasn't smiling. "You ever seen his backyard? That pile of junk is surely full of rats, and if it ever catches fire, places all around it'll burn."

"I'll bet," said Charles, "that you've never really talked to him, heard what he—"

"Excuse me! If you—how'd you put it?—'want to know the real story,' I went to high school with Dexter, until he dropped out. Couldn't hardly spell his name, let alone do math or—"

"Could hardly."

198

"What?" And then sharply, "Were you *correcting* me?! Robert, your boy here . . . they better teach him some manners at that university he's going to."

The judge, clearly wanting to lighten the mood, said, "I think Charles has a soft spot for these men on the street crew. Nothing wrong with that." But Charles had already headed for the door, not bothering to say goodbye. His father followed him out, walking with him to the end of the café's green-striped awning.

"Junior shouldn't have said that, but I don't think he meant any harm. He's just blowing off, being Junior. At least he knows who Dexter is."

"Yeah, knows just enough about him to make fun of his dream about the Ozarks. That's not right, you know that's not right, and you let him get away with it! Just like you let Sheriff Wood get away with things."

His father took a deep breath, looked at the wet sidewalk, and then directly at Charles. "You will go off to school and, chances are, move to some big city where you can pick and choose your friends. But *this* is where I live. *These* are my friends, and likely will be for the rest of my life. So when you get to Drake, you can join all the moral crusades you want. But while you are here, living in my house, you will be civil to my friends."

In fact, they didn't do much work the rest of Tuesday. Clyde wasn't there when Charles returned to the garage, and the rain

199

only got steadier. Clyde wasn't there on Wednesday either, but, since the rain had stopped, the three of them agreed that Moss and Charles would clean out the storm drains, while Dexter repaired and reset three Stop signs that badly needed it.

At first, they drove the old pickup from drain to drain in unusual silence, Moss obviously preoccupied. Angry at Clyde? Worried about Clyde? At one point, Charles spoke of his intention, henceforth, to use the name Jim, but Moss, with a wave of his hand, said not to bother. "'What's in a name?' By now, everybody calls me Moss. But I know who I am, I guess."

Then, after another lengthy silence, Charles asked if they were going to clean out the storm drain on the square in front of the bank. "We don't do that one," said Moss.

"Why not?"

Moss cracked his knuckles on the steering wheel as he stopped the truck near a badly clogged drain. "Well, it seems that Clyde and Clarence, the old man whose family started that bank, had a fight."

Charles shook his head. "We just let it overflow because of that? What was the fight about?"

"Dexter thinks it's because the old man, back when he was on the city council, when he *was* the city council, wouldn't vote to spend more money on the streets. And it's true. He's always been against spending money on new equipment, or on much of anything. But from what Clyde said one time, I think it's more personal. I think Clarence wouldn't give Clyde a loan so his girl could start college. But I won't swear to that."

Charles mulled over this news, this speculation, as they scooped up sludge and threw it on top of other debris in the bed of the pickup. As they were getting back in the cab, he said, "Speaking of daughters, how is Callie doing? We haven't talked about her since that day at the dump."

Moss stared out the open side window. Finally, as he turned the ignition, he mumbled, more to himself than to Charles, "'How sharper than a serpent's tooth,'" and Charles knew better than to ask what he meant.

Since it was Wednesday, Frankie wouldn't be free that evening, but after work Charles dropped by Fashion on the Square to say a quick hello. Frankie was with a customer, with two more waiting, so he waved, blew her a kiss when he thought the others weren't looking (although, with all the mirrors it was hard to tell), and stepped back out on the sidewalk. Now what? At home, his mother would just bug him about packing for his big departure. So, on the spur of the moment, he decided to swing by the church.

The secretary was already gone for the day, and Reverend Shelton was on the phone. But when Charles stuck his head in the door marked "Pastor's Study," the minister stood up and motioned for him to come in.

"Yes, I will be sure to look into it." Long pause, the voice on the other end of the line so loud Charles could hear it from his side of the desk, though he couldn't make out the words. He scanned the rows of books on both sides of the east-facing window, as well as the memorabilia: a baseball with a single signature; an old pocket watch dangling under a dome; an award for something in the shape of a tractor, all scattered here and there on the shelves. Finally, Reverend Shelton was able to say, "Why don't I come by later this week, and we can discuss it further." Another pause, during which he rolled his eyes, and they both smiled. "Okay, I will. Goodbye."

"That," he said as he put down the receiver, "is a fan of yours. Mrs. Cunningham has told me at least three times how you and Jerry hauled away the tree limb that was blocking her driveway. Because she was able to get out of her drive, she was able to help Mrs. Atkins get her groceries so she could have her niece over for a meal. You tipped a whole row of dominoes. She seems to think it wasn't even part of your job." He came around the desk to a chair closer to where Charles was sitting. "I hope she thanked you directly."

"Yes, she gave us lemonade."

"And probably one of her pictures." They both smiled again as Charles nodded.

"Before you tell me why you stopped in, and I'm really glad you did, and before I forget to mention it, Reverend Miller told me he saw you at his church. It must have been at one of his Wednesday prayer services. Although, I guess it could have been on a Sunday morning," he said smiling.

"How do you know him?" asked Charles.

"Doesn't your dad know all the lawyers in the area? Lionel Miller and I are colleagues, and friends. We actually have a lot in common. Like, we're both from Iowa, although I grew up on a farm and he's from Des Moines." He smiled broadly, probably at Charles' raised eyebrows. "Things aren't always what you expect, are they?"

"But that church is so . . . different. It's like I was in another country."

"Nope," said Reverend Shelton, "you were in Savannah County, all right. But it's true that sometimes you can leave home, leave the 'castle,' without ever crossing the county line." He settled back in his chair. "I imagine you were there with Frankie. Can I ask how that's going?"

"I like being with her," said Charles quickly. "She's different, too. Like, she's never even been to the pool or the Country Club." When the minister remained silent, he added, "Everyone seems to know we've been seeing each other. So I thought," he paused "maybe you could tell me what people are saying."

"Do you really care what . . . ?" Reverend Shelton stopped and then nodded. "Fair enough. I suppose people, at least at this church, those who stick their nose in such things, don't think she's your type." He laughed. "But I suppose people in her church don't think you're *her* type." He leaned forward in the chair and looked more serious. "I think Frankie's a special young

203

woman with lots of strength. If she came to see me, I'd tell her to be careful of getting too involved with you."

Charles really wanted to know why he would say this, but that felt too defensive, so instead he asked, "How do you know her? Clyde and Frankie aren't in our church."

"My ministry is to Savannah County. It just happens that some of its residents belong to this congregation, which I *am* happy about, because they're the ones who pay my salary." Again, smiling.

Charles pondered this while the reverend got up and poured them each a cup of thick coffee from the bottom of the small glass pot sitting on the credenza behind his desk. When he returned, Charles asked, "If you're the minister to the whole county, do you know what's the story with Callie Moss? Has she had . . . has she been pregnant?"

Now it was Reverend Shelton's turn to raise his eyebrows. "Sorry. You'll need to ask her or her father about that."

"Do you know her father's first name?"

Another smile, this time squinting his eyes before saying, "That's a great question, and I think it's Jim." They sipped the nearly undrinkable coffee. Charles was about to ask if he knew whether Moss had taught in the country school or the reason for the fight between Clyde and Clarence the banker, but it was Reverend Shelton who next spoke. "From what I can see, you've enjoyed these months working with the street crew."

"What I don't get," said Charles, "is why people talk about them like they're stupid and lazy. We put asphalt in holes, like you're supposed to do. Then it gets scooped out by the weather and people driving on it, which is just what happens, and the street crew gets blamed for it. We tar the road because people complain about the dust, and then they complain about how we tar them. I know you say people are basically good, but it seems to me that most people like running other people down." The minister nodded, but said nothing. "That's another way Frankie's church is different from ours. You preach that people are good, he preaches that they're not. At least when I was there he did."

"Well," said Reverend Shelton, "sometimes I actually talk about evil, because there is evil in the world and it's important for us to recognize it; and I'm sure there are times when Lionel preaches about the goodness in us, because that's also true. People need to hear—are ready to hear—different messages in the different seasons of their lives." He took another sip of coffee and winced. "But in any case, I'm sorry some local folks have been disparaging your friends on the street crew."

"My mother doesn't run them down exactly," said Charles, "but she doesn't think working on the street crew was the right way to get ready for college."

"I don't like to contradict your mother," said Reverend Shelton, "but I can't imagine a better preparation."

*****

205

Since Clyde was still absent from work, Charles spent a good part of Thursday finishing his survey of Lockwood's gravel streets, including one near Billy's Auto Parts that was completely new to him. How could that be? How could he forget being on a street in a town no bigger than this?

On Friday, his final day, as the three of them congregated around the couch, word came from the secretary in the city office that water, a lot of it, was running down a street near the hospital. They squeezed into the pickup, Charles in the middle, and drove the twelve blocks to where water was bubbling from the base of a neglected-looking fire hydrant.

"Seems like it's broke over there," said Moss, motioning toward a soggy patch of grass. "At least it's an empty lot."

Dexter considered the scene while puffing on his pipe, and finally nodded. "Let's get the water shut off an' dig 'er up."

"I'll take you to fetch the tractor," said Moss, but Dexter shook his head.

"Charlie here can drive it, bein' it's his last day."

And so, after being dropped off at the garage, Charles bounced and jolted the twelve blocks to the broken water pipe, the scoop like the head of some mythical beast on whose back he was riding, the backhoe sticking out behind like a tail. Past the grade school, where kids were playing Wiffle ball, past his church (which was only a block out of the way), past the 7-Eleven (which was only another block in the wrong direction), then back and up the slight hill with water flowing past him to

206

where Dexter and Moss were leaning on the pickup, the hospital on his left, the vacant lot on his right.

Charles gunned the tractor over the curb and positioned the backhoe near the soggy ground. "You want to do this, Dexter?" he shouted over the roar.

"Nope, you do it. Keep 'er not too deep 'til we see what's doin'."

Charles manipulated the levers of the backhoe, as Clyde had briefly taught him, scooping up the grass and top soil until there was a trench, Dexter and Moss hauling out the water that pooled in it. "Now what?" he shouted, but it wasn't clear Dexter could hear him.

After lifting another bucket of water from the trench, Dexter gestured with his pipe. "Down that a way some."

Extend the trench? Charles wasn't sure of the instruction, but he backed the tractor away from the edge of the hole, turning it toward the slightly tilted hydrant. When, however, he started in that direction, with more of a lurch than intended, the saturated soil gave way and the tractor was stuck, the mud nearly to the top of its tires. They tried pulling it out with the empty dump truck, and when that didn't work, it took a couple of hours to get the state crew to fill the truck with gravel.

"This'll do 'er," said Dexter, while Moss cracked his knuckles and Charles felt slightly sick to his stomach. But when they got back to the site, two cars were parked close enough to the hydrant that they couldn't get the large dump truck in place.

They checked the nearby houses, but either no one was home or the cars weren't theirs.

"Probably someone in the hospital," said Moss. "Doesn't seem right to have them towed if they're visiting patients."

And so they waited, the sun moving steadily to the west, Charles spending the time trying to imagine his first day at Drake and, even more, his last day with Frankie. Finally, when it was clear that neither Dexter nor Moss would do it, Charles entered the hospital and had the friendly woman at the information desk page the owners of the two cars, who promptly and gladly responded. As he was exiting the hospital's main entrance, Charles saw Clyde and his wife leaving by another door—Clyde hunched, his arm across his abdomen. And when he got back to the truck, he could tell that Dexter and Moss had seen them, too.

They pulled the tractor out of the muck, and set up caution signs around the open trench, without speaking. Charles had envisioned a sad but joyful departure, a chance to tell Dexter and Moss . . . well, he wasn't quite sure what he wanted to tell them; but, in any case, it didn't happen. When they got back to the garage—Dexter driving the dump truck, Moss the tractor, Charles the pickup—the older men seemed preoccupied. Finally, Moss said, "Good luck in college." Dexter nodded and that was that.

*****

Charles told Frankie he wanted to spend all day Saturday with her—all weekend, for that matter—and she agreed, as long as he knew she would be in church for two or three hours on Sunday. He suggested that he pick her up at her home around 10:00 on Saturday morning. She said, "Make it 11:00, and I'll meet you on the west side of the square."

Charles envisioned driving to Lake Winyan and, since Frankie liked to hike, walking beside her on one of the heavily-wooded trails, where they would be alone to talk, although, once again, he wasn't sure what he wanted to say. That he hoped she would come to Des Moines for special weekends? That he would like to see her whenever he could get back to Lockwood? That it would probably be too hard to keep something going at a distance, so maybe . . . But she said, "Let's go to Mahaska and see an afternoon movie," and he agreed.

He suggested they see a film that had just come out, called "The Graduate," but Frankie seemed reluctant, so they settled on another new one, "Bonnie and Clyde," sharing a bag of popcorn she insisted on paying for. When it was over, she said something about wanting to see the new Bond movie, and so they also watched "You Only Live Twice," kissing occasionally, especially during the sexier scenes, Charles' arm around her shoulders, Frankie's hand on his leg. They left the theater a little after 7:00.

Impulsively, Charles suggested they drive to the restaurant overlooking the river near Red Rock, see if they could get a table

209

without a reservation, like they had way back in July. But even he wasn't sure this was such a great idea; and so, when Frankie said, "I'd rather just get a sandwich here in Mahaska," he agreed.

Her next request caught him completely off guard. "On the way back to Lockwood, let's go by that burned church. You never did show me where you found the body."

"Really? You want to see it? You never seemed all that interested. In fact, you asked me less about it than just about anybody."

"Charles, everyone in town was making a big fuss over it. You didn't need me treating you like some kind of celebrity, did you?"

And so, of course, he agreed. But by the time they finished eating loose-meat hamburgers—pickles, no onions—in a crowded downtown diner, it was nearly dark, and Charles began to feel a bit uneasy. He and Jerry had had a difficult enough time finding Mars Hill in the daylight. Could he find it at night? Could he remember Clyde's directions?

South on Highway 19 to the Turner Road, which, it turns out, is completely unmarked coming from the north. Thankfully, he recognized it and headed east, turning left on the third gravel road. This, however, didn't feel right, and after a mile or so he turned around. The moon was three-quarters full, and when it was out from behind the clouds, they could see cornfields on the flat bottom land, surrounded by hills dense with trees, but it kept flickering in and out of the clouds, leaving them at times in deep darkness.

He tried the fourth gravel road, another mile or more down the Turner Road, the turn nearly hidden by a large tree, and things began to feel more familiar. Across the short bridge, the Buick's headlights reflecting off the sign that warned of high water, jogging left where the road split. This was truly the hilliest corner of the county, and when the moon escaped the cloud cover, they could see fingers of forest reaching down the hillsides into the cultivated land.

Charles started to say they weren't far from where a farmer killed his wife (maybe) and then shot himself, but thought better of it. And so they drove in silence past the jagged-edged cornfields, the stalks nearly twice the height of the car, around the big curve and past the only farmhouse in sight, its porch light shining like a beacon at sea. Then up the steeply-sloping hill, trees so close in places that their branches overhung part of the road, the big car's tires crunching on the loose gravel. Frankie placed her hand on his leg, high on his leg, on the inside of his leg, and moved closer. Not for the first time he was glad the Buick didn't have a Mustang's bucket seats.

They rounded the last curve and pulled into the cleared area in front of what remained of the old log church: one wall and a small part of another, the edges charred and jagged. Charles turned off the engine, but kept the lights on, illuminating the ruin in front of them. Shadows from gently swaying trees flitted

211

across the scene as the moon moved in and out of the clouds. He started to speak, but then they both sat listening intently to the crunch of gravel as a car sped around the curve, slowed nearly to a stop, and finally drove on by. Charles realized he had been squeezing Frankie's hand, and vice versa. She let out a deep breath and almost giggled.

They sat quietly for a minute, two minutes, both listening for the sound of gravel. Finally, when it didn't come, Charles said, "It was in that area to the right, quite a ways back in those trees, that I found the body. Like I told you, I was pushing the wheelbarrow toward a big rock. It was—"

Frankie reached across him and pushed in a knob, turning off the lights. The moon was bright enough now that he could see her face—her eyes, her neck, the tops of her breasts—as she said, "You've been wanting to fuck me for the last two months. So, let's do it."

Yes! Wasn't this the stuff of his daydreams? Isn't this what he'd been imagining for their last weekend? But why, then, was he suddenly so nervous, his heart thumping in his chest? "Here?" he said, his voice catching in his throat.

"Well, I don't think you're gonna do anything wild and crazy like get a motel room, so we'll just do it here." She smiled and ran her fingers through the hair on his temple. "Don't you think we'll fit in the back seat? I've seen a lot smaller seats than this one."

He wanted to ask if that meant she'd done this before, but a voice in his head told him that wasn't wise because he might not like the answer. He thought of the condom still squished in his wallet, but what he said was, "I don't have any protection."

Frankie had already opened the front passenger-side door and was taking off her blouse. "It's taken care of."

Charles slipped off his shirt and jeans in the front seat. By the time he climbed out and opened the back door of the Buick, she was already naked, stretched out as much as she could, with her legs toward him. Her breasts, now that he saw them like this, were even more prominent—more wonderful!—than he had imagined. And her legs, dimly lit by the moon . . . . He was pleased to feel the sight of her having an effect, but was it normal to be so nervous? In his fantasies, he was always the one in control. After all, Nancy didn't know any more about sex than he did, but now . . . "You surprised me," he told her. "I thought you didn't want to since I'm going off to school."

Frankie sighed and raised up on her elbows, and again he could see her eyes. "Charles! Are you really going to have a debate about this?" She laughed. "Sometimes I feel ten years older than you, not just two." He could see her smile, her gentle, wonderful smile, with no hint of mockery. "I've been making things too complicated in my own mind, so let's not make them complicated now. Okay? Even if you . . . even if we don't know what we're doing, we'll figure it out."

He started to get in the backseat, then stepped out to pull off his briefs, and got back in, closing the door behind him. "Roll that window down," said Frankie. "It'll be too stuffy, maybe even steamy, if we're good." Charles reached behind and awkwardly cranked the window, until Frankie laughed again, said "that's good enough," and pulled him on top of her, with one hand behind his head, the other behind his rear. Her body smashed against his like at the fair, only now it was front to front, skin against skin—her legs, her stomach, her breasts, pressed against him in a way he had never experienced. He felt himself growing harder, his tension giving way to pure, glorious passion—all of which changed in an instant with a loud pounding on the driver's side of the car. Charles jerked up and could almost feel the flashlight moving along his spine, until it was shining on Frankie's face, and then on her one exposed breast.

"Well, well. I guessed it was you, little girl, before I looked in the window. Who you whorin' with this time?" The light swung around to Charles who was trying awkwardly to sit up. "If it isn't Moss' little buddy."

"Shut up, Woody!" said Frankie. "We weren't doing anything—anything wrong."

"I wonder," said the sheriff, the light now roaming across her torso, "if that's how your daddy will see it. It'll be a shame to tell him how his daughter still fucks around, with him bein' sick as he is."

214

For some reason, Charles found himself wondering why he hadn't heard the sound of gravel, but finally he spoke. "I know what my dad means when he says you're a bastard!"

"Does he now? That's something comin' from a lawyer who makes his money kicking old ladies out of their apartments."

Charles started to respond, words jumbling in his head, when the sheriff cut him off. "Let's see if I have it straight. College kid comes back in the middle of the night to the place where drugs were bein' made and someone was killed. College kid has had a chance to clean up the place, maybe get rid of evidence. College kid even knows where to find the body, hidden way out in the woods. I wonder if there's a connection. People may begin to wonder about it, too."

By now, Frankie had wriggled out from under Charles and there was enough moonlight that he could see the rage on her face, and hear it in her voice. "Leave him alone!"—her shout, her *scream*, ringing across the hilltop. And then, in a much lower voice: "I know how this works." As Charles watched, she opened the back door of the Buick, scooped up her clothes without putting them on, and walked gingerly over the gravel to the patrol car that was parked, nearly invisible, in the shadow of a giant oak.

"Run on home, sonny," said the sheriff, clicking off the flashlight, "and maybe I'll forget you were here."

215

Chapter Ten

The road from Des Moines to Lockwood isn't a roller coaster like the roads in Savannah County, but Charles still loved this drive, even in the middle of winter. He loved the look of fields with a stubble of corn stalks, red barns, their roofs coated white, bare trees scattered along the hedge rows. This, he knew, would be part of him, wherever he ended up.

There were various routes he could take and still make the drive in under two hours. He could go east out of Des Moines, and then straight south on Highway 19 to Mahaska and Lockwood. He could go south out of Des Moines before picking up Highway 52, then east into Lockwood, avoiding Mahaska altogether. On this day, however, he had decided to go southeast, through New Holland and White Cloud, on smaller roads that run parallel to the Des Moines River on its meandering way to Savannah County. This route is more direct, but there was a good chance of getting stuck behind a truck or a tractor with several cars in a row impatiently waiting their moment to zip past when the yellow line disappears. Whenever he was stuck in such a line, especially if stacked up behind a semi, Charles thought of his grandparents. What had run through their minds in that instant before the truck demolished their car? You can plan for the future, but who knows what's in store. Sometimes people don't seem to be blessed or lucky.

His family, including his grandparents, occasionally had stopped in New Holland for Dutch pastries at the little bakery on the square near the town's tourist attraction windmill. He liked driving through this town, but, even more, he liked driving past the three-story house, with its round upper windows, standing alone in the countryside between New Holland and White Cloud, that had been part of the Underground Railroad. Or so his father, the amateur historian, had told him. According to his dad, there is a tunnel from the cellar of the house to the bank of a nearby stream, in case former slaves had needed to get away quickly. There must be so many secret histories, he mused, in every field, around every bend—whole other worlds that would remain mysteries to him. Like whatever happened with that farmer and his wife. Like whatever happened in the old log church.

Charles learned that Clyde had died from his father, who mentioned it almost in passing during their Sunday phone conversation. No, that wasn't accurate. His father knew Clyde was important to him, just not how important. Maybe it wasn't even Clyde, Charles reflected, but the whole experience of which Clyde was an integral part. In any case, as soon as his father told him the funeral would be Tuesday at 1:30, he knew he had to go. And he knew he wouldn't tell his family he was going.

It certainly wasn't a convenient time. Drake had been in session three weeks since Christmas break, so all four of his courses had exams upcoming or papers due in the next few days, and two of his classes met on Tuesday. But he had lined up friends to take notes, and no snow was predicted, so he could be back, if all went well, by dinner time. Well, since it was a Pentecostal service, things might go a bit longer, but at least some time that evening.

The road took him past farmhouses, most painted white, many with tilted mailboxes and drainage ditches filled with tall, cattail-like weeds out front. He had called Jerry right after hearing from his father, although they never managed to speak directly. Charles left a message with someone in Jerry's fraternity; and when Jerry called back on Monday, he had to leave a message with someone in Charles' residence hall: "Sorry to hear about Clyde. Too much going on to get away, but you are better at that kind of thing, anyway. Give my regards to Frankie."

Ah yes, Frankie. Charles hadn't gone home for his high school homecoming, and when he returned to Lockwood for Thanksgiving and Christmas, he spent the entire time with family. He had intended to stop by Fashion on the Square during the week after Christmas—just to say hello, just to see how she was, just to say . . . But the days slipped by, and he never

219

managed to get to Fashion on the Square. In fact, he returned early to Drake because of his job in the library. Or so he told himself.

There had been talk of him needing to return to Lockwood in order to testify at an inquest, but no one was ever charged with a crime in connection with the Mars Hill fire, and the idea of an inquest was dropped. The official story—which, again, he heard from his father—was that the young man had been badly burned in an explosion he caused while mixing methamphetamine, and then dragged himself into the trees where he died. Although why he would drag himself there, or how he might actually manage it given the severity of his burns, was never fully explained. While Charles was still working in Lockwood, the boy's mother, without much notice in the *Republican* or the *Democrat*, had come from Memphis to identify the body. Later on, she apparently raised a fuss about the investigation; but nothing came of it, and the town moved on. Charles knew there was something fundamentally wrong with the whole affair, but to whom would he make his complaint? And, beside, he too was moving on.

Memory of this tragedy led him to think of that night at Mars Hill. As he drove past frozen ponds and stubbled fields, Charles could picture himself steering his Buick toward the patrol car until their bumpers touched, his high beams lighting up the sheriff like a scared deer, then laying on his horn until he could hear the crunch of tires as a neighbor approached along the gravel road. But that's what he now wished he had done, not what he actually did. He *had* called out to Frankie, but she never looked back before sliding into the sheriff's cruiser. And then he had driven away, nursing a guilty rage, back down the hill, back past the fork in the road, back across the bridge with its warning sign, back to the highway that carried him back to Lockwood, where he told no one.

There had been few trucks or tractors blocking his way, so Charles arrived at Hope of the World Pentecostal Church several minutes early. He intended to take a seat toward the rear, but then, there was Frankie, in a plain black dress, standing alone inside the entrance, off to one side. She looked up and seemed surprised as he hesitantly headed her way.

"Your school have a break?"

"I came for the funeral." He started to add *and to see you,* but they both would know that wasn't quite true. Her eyes (how could he forget those eyes) were fixed intently on him, but her look was gentle. "I'm really sorry," he said, "about Clyde."

"He liked you a lot, Charles. In his own peculiar way." She smiled, and so did he. "Anyway, he walks now with Jesus, and that's a blessing."

Charles wasn't sure what to say to this, so asked, "Did the cancer just get worse and worse until his body gave out?"

"Actually," said Frankie, "his spirit gave out first. You may not know that he killed himself, or at least we think he did. It's not a secret, but we're also not advertising it, especially here. The church just pretends it didn't happen, just sticks to saying 'he's in a better place.'"

Charles' face revealed his shock, and she put her hand on his arm. "Mom really wasn't too surprised. She said she knew how he hated the idea of being a burden to anybody. What I think is that, after all those years of being so strong, he couldn't stand being weak."

"So, did you . . . find him?"

She pulled her hand back and shook her head. "Dexter found him in the garage on Saturday. They'd stopped going in on Saturdays, budget cuts or something. But Dexter needed to go there for some reason, and that's when he found him, already dead for a while."

Frankie turned away to receive condolences from several people. When she turned back, Charles said, "I'm sorry I didn't get to say goodbye to Clyde, but," he fumbled with the funeral bulletin in his hand, "I'm also sorry we, I mean you and me, never got to say goodbye, or—"

She put her finger to his lips, gently. "Charles, let's not talk about any of that, okay? You just say, 'Frankie, how pretty you look,' and I say, 'Charles, how sweet of you to come for Clyde's funeral.'"

Her brother, Scott, walked up, stared at Charles (not gently), and then walked on. Frankie's face brightened. "I'll tell you something fun. I'm taking a course over at the community

222

college in Centerville, just to try it out. See if I'm cut out for doing more studying. Your friend, Kenny, came in the store one day, and he's the one who told me it's a good school; so I decided to give it a try. Clyde put a little money aside, I guess in case I wanted to."

"That's great, Frankie! What are you taking?"

She looked down and smiled. "You'll laugh."

"Only if it's a course in fashion merchandising."

He expected her to laugh, but she said simply, "History. European history."

It was getting close to 1:30, and more people were coming in, but Frankie seemed unconcerned about the time, and they continued to talk. Yes, he was enjoying Drake; and, yes, it was challenging; although, yes, he was doing well in his courses. Yes, working at Fashion on the Square was getting old; yes, she had her eye out for another job; and, yes, she liked his hair longer. "You look like you're really fitting in." They asked no questions about dating.

"I'm sure my parents won't be here," Charles told her. "And I don't plan on going by my dad's house, my parent's house, while I'm in town."

"I don't imagine anyone from the city council will be here," said Frankie, but not with bitterness. "They had a party for him when he had to quit working. I think they thought they said goodbye to him then. Besides, who wants to come all the way out here to a crummy Pentecostal church, anyway? A person would have to be out of his mind to drive all the way here from Des Moines!" Again, that smile.

The idea came to him unbidden, and he voiced it before further thinking could drive it away. "As I remember," trying to sound casual, off-hand, "the New York City Ballet is coming to Des Moines the weekend after next. And I was wondering if . . . in fact, that's the date . . . I'll have to check, but I'm pretty sure it is . . . if you'd like to go." His mouth felt parched, and he was sure his ears were red enough to betray him. "You know, I could drive down . . . it's not all that far, not more than a couple of hours . . . and pick you up. Maybe for the weekend, or if that wouldn't work . . ."

Her eyes were blurry as she reached up on tiptoe and kissed him tenderly on the cheek. "Bye, Charles." They were suddenly engulfed in a late-arriving group, and by the time it cleared, she was seated next to her mother, both of them crying, in the front of the church.

The funeral service didn't get started nearly on time (something Frankie obviously anticipated), and so it wasn't over until well after 3:00. Charles lingered in the back, watching for Frankie, but she apparently slipped out by a side door. When he finally left the church, he saw Moss, standing alone, and went to greet him.

"We all must 'shuffle off this mortal coil,'" said Moss, "but I know he suffered a lot, until he took care of it himself. That's Clyde for you."

224

"Dexter didn't come?"

"He told me he'd already said farewell. Well, actually he didn't say much of anything, but I know he thought he'd already said it."

They stood awkwardly for a minute, Charles glancing around to see if, by some chance, Frankie might be coming his way, before he asked, "Is Dexter now the head of the street crew?"

"Didn't your dad tell you? Well, I see why he wouldn't. The city council, in their wisdom, decided to bring in a retired farmer from Ponca County, named Bill Colglazer—Colblazer, Bill Col-something—to run the street crew. Seems no one thought Dexter, or me, for that matter, could do it."

And so, contrary to his plan, Charles drove into Lockwood, avoiding the north side of the square, parking in the alley behind the city garage. By the time he got there, it was getting close to 4:30. Dexter, in his usual perch on the edge of the workbench, did not seem particularly surprised to see him. Bill, who was in Clyde's place on the couch, introduced himself to Charles without getting up. Glancing around, Charles could see the garage looked the same, except that under the windows sat Dexter's piano—uncovered, an ashtray resting on the top, cobwebs hanging from under the keyboard.

"I came for Clyde's funeral," said Charles, looking at Dexter, "and thought I'd just stop by to say hello, especially since I didn't see you there."

225

Dexter took a puff before saying, "Guess I'm not much for funerals, for wearing ties an' such." But he looked sad.

"Could you see it coming, Dexter? I mean, was he getting more depressed or whatever?"

A puff. "I reckon we could of if we'd knowed what we was lookin' for."

"Is it true, what I heard, that you found him . . . here?"

Charles could hear the old clock tick off the seconds before Dexter said, "Yep. He was under that old sand spreader, over yonder by them shelves." He gestured with his pipe. "They say he tied a rope to it—used that ol' extension ladder, I reckon—an' pulled the spreader off that shelf way up there on his head." A puff. "Caved it in purdy good, surely did."

Charles felt queasiness in his stomach as he pictured the scene. Finally, he asked, "What do you think happened?"

Dexter leaned forward. "Maybe he was goin' to show hisself he could still lift it."

Charles wasn't sure how much more he wanted to know about the suicide, so after a pause and more ticks of the clock, he said, "It seems like a long time ago that I was here."

"Well," said Bill, "let me see. I been here—what's it been, Dexter?—three or four months. You fill a few holes, blade a few roads, then it's winter and you shovel some snow. Things keep a movin', don't they, Dexter?" No one spoke, until Bill said, "Well, I'm movin', too," as he extracted himself slowly from the couch. "You take care now," and he left, without a glance at Dexter who sat smoking on the bench.

They were silent for a minute, but it was a comfortable silence, punctuated by the ticking of the clock. Finally, Charles said, "You were right. The Cardinals did win the pennant. And the World Series, too."

"Yep, they did," said Dexter with a brown, jagged smile. "They surely did." He sat smoking for a minute before he asked, "You studyin' that history like you said?"

"I don't think that'll be my major subject," said Charles. "Once I got there, other things seemed more interesting." Dexter nodded and puffed.

Then Charles told him about the funeral, and how the minister compared Clyde to a cactus, all prickly on the outside, but a lot sweeter than he wanted people to know on the inside. Dexter nodded, his gaze in the distance, as Charles spoke. "Reverend Miller also said that, while Clyde could seem really gruff, he was a loving father who wanted the best for his kids, including a chance for them to go to college. And I know for a fact that's true." Dexter rocked on the workbench as he nodded.

"Do you have a church you go to, Dexter?"

One puff. Two puffs. "Wife does. I go with 'er some."

"Where does she, where do you, go?"

Two puffs. "Out in the county . . . near Stiles."

"What kind of church is it?"

Ten seconds. Fifteen. "Just a church." Then after a puff, "Good people. Knowed her all her life. Come by when she's sickly. Just not many of 'em anymore."

They sat in silence for a while, until Charles said, "I learned a lot last summer from you and Clyde."

This time Dexter responded faster. "An' Jim."

Charles smiled. "And Jim. From all three of you. Running the tractor, using a grease gun, mixing cement."

"I reckon," said Dexter, "a feller can get on in life without knowin' any a that." And this time they both smiled.

"I won't forget that time Clyde put the truck in second while Jerry and I were shoveling sand like mad men." Dexter rocked and smiled and nodded. "Or when I ripped the track off that door frame with the tractor bucket."

Dexter raised his chin as if in thought. "I remember," he said quietly, "when you boys come by my house." Comfortable silence.

"So how are things around here, I mean after Clyde?"

"It ain't too bad. 'Course I hated to see Clyde go, I surely did. But I knowed he was gettin' tired. Yes, sir. Real tired."

"And what about you, Dexter? What have you been doing for yourself these past months?"

Ten seconds. Fifteen. "Not much." A puff. "But me an' the wife is plannin' to go to the Ozarks this year. Soon as it gets warm." Another puff. "We was goin' last summer, but she got too sickly." He took the pipe from his mouth and laid it beside him on the bench. "Yep, that's right. Soon as it gets warm."

About the Author

Michael Kinnamon, a native of Iowa, is a former professor of Christian theology, author of several nonfiction books, and highly regarded as a scholar in the field of ecumenical and interfaith studies. He is the former General Secretary of the National Council of Churches, headquartered in Washington, DC. He lives with his wife, Mardine Davis, in San Diego. This is his debut novel.

Acknowledgments

I am deeply grateful for the encouragement and direction given me by Publerati's publisher, Caleb Mason. His careful, patient, wise editorial advice has made this a better novel.

I am thankful for the friends—including Lydia, Ron A., Joe, Ron K., and Brian—who read early drafts of *Summer of Love and Evil* and provided helpful, encouraging feedback.

It was my wife, Mardine, who urged me, when I had completed one career, a career largely centered in my head, to take up another, this one more centered in my heart. My Ph.D. in Religion and Literature was a stepping stone to a satisfying career in theological studies. The "literature" part of that degree, however, has always been a crucial dimension of my life, and I have long had a desire to be a writer of fiction, not simply a reader and teacher of it. Mardine's amazing support has now made that desire a reality.